SECOND WIND

SECOND WIND

MINAL ARORA

Ocean Books Pvt. Ltd.
ISO 9001:2015 Publishers

Published by
Ocean Books (P) Ltd.
4/19 Asaf Ali Road,
New Delhi-110 002 (INDIA)
e-mail: info@oceanbooks.in

ISBN 978-81-8430-578-4
SECOND WIND
by Minal Arora

Cover Painting
Eva Urbaníková

Paperback edition
First, 2020

Price
₹ 350.00 (Rupees Three Hundred Fifty only)

Printed at
R-Tech Offset Printers, Delhi

This journey is dedicated to the men in my life. My father, my son, my mate, my brother and numerous others, who inadvertently revealed to me the diverse shades of the masculine within.

It is the wisdom of the masculine that manifested into the words that flowed through me as this book.

Contents

	Acknowledgements	*9*
	Author's Note	*11*
1.	Bygones	15
2.	The Quest	21
3.	Divine Intervention	36
4.	In La La Land	45
5.	Healing Cottage	56
6.	The Encounter	67
7.	The Bali Escapade	80
8.	Back Home	163
9.	The Final Straw	185
10.	Second Wind	191

Acknowledgements

For this book, my deepest acknowledgment to **Ritu Sharma** for helping me by re-reading this book over and over, till it felt right. She not only edited the manuscript twice but counselled me on aspects where I needed a friend's perspective. Thank you Ritu for your unconditional love and support. Your ability to accept the work entrusted to you while never letting your smile fade away is something that inspires me. Thank you for the late-night discussions and the beautiful, insightful suggestions you always poured in, to add value to my books.

Cynthia Roli Gupta was the first person I sent the script to, in 2018, when it was fresh out of the alleys of my mind, on paper, ready to be reviewed. I waited with bated breath for her feedback was important to me, considering she knew Maaya as well as I did, and this was Rahul's story. Her appreciation for the book and subsequently being the first one to edit it, played a big role in how the story came to be shaped.

Thank you **Barnali** for your final touches to editing the book and getting it ready for life.

I cannot miss acknowledging my family, starting with

my parents, my son Sanat, my sisters Shilpi and Sheetal, their hubbies Vineet and Vikas and the kiddos Aadi, Ansh, Abir and Sophie. They all contribute to making my life worth living and thus worth sharing through my books. Thank you, dear family.

Author's Note

If you are reading Second Wind, then either you have already read 'Maaya: A tryst with Self', or you will be compelled to read it after following Rahul on his journey through this book. When I penned the story of Maaya in 2014, I was very unsure of why I was doing it. It seemed as if some lost pearls from my own life, some spilled by my clients about theirs, some tattered expressions suffocated deep within, all had found a place in that book. With ample divine guidance coming my way, it felt like Maaya had a role to play in the lives of several others who saw themselves in her. In the coming few years when I received long heart-warming letters and confessions from people from different parts of the country and sometimes across borders, conveying how Maaya touched them deeply, my eyes would well up. I have always wondered what I might have done in my past lives to have deserved so much love and acceptance from everyone around me. All this inspires me to strive each day to be better than yesterday for I want to bask in all this love, contain it, hold it and imbibe it.

Second Wind happened to reveal itself completely just a week before the launch of INFiNITY, my second book which is a non-fictional book. At the time, I was concerned that while I should really be preparing for my second book's launch, I was instead busy finishing my third. This wasn't because of greed. It's just that these books seem to have a mind of their own. Anyone who truly writes from what comes to them from deep within will know, it's not a process one can control from the mind. The book would reveal itself to me whenever I was ready to receive the next bit. I don't think through about what I plan to write. It just happens to write itself through me and all I must do is allow it to come through. To imagine and write Second Wind would have been extremely challenging because the nuances of the masculine mind that are explored through Rahul are not what I would as a woman be able to experience or convey had I not trusted my guidance from within.

My only urge to you as a reader is to be open, accepting and generous while walking with Rahul for that is what his journey is all about—liberation from his own limiting perceptions to enable him to be to what he must be. It was only after writing this book that I realized that it will be a trilogy and there will be a third book coming. Maaya was written during 2011-2014 and Second Wind was written in 2018. I was not expecting the third part to show up anytime soon but to my surprise it is. As I type this note, the third part is on its way and I have already written a few chapters of it. It should be out sometime in 2021.

It amazes me as to how these books have presented some deep aspects of life and relationships, always staying focused on the light behind everything. I am grateful to each one of you who have walked with me on this path and have written to me, talked to me or in any other way conveyed your love for my work and its relevance in your lives. That's how I continue, knowing that someone somewhere will find the seed of their life in this story and for their sake, I must say it.

Thank you for your love and kindness. I feel eternally grateful.

Bygones

It was the darkest of nights. Even the stars seemed to be hiding behind a wall of foreboding clouds. The chill in the air hurt so deep that it was difficult to breathe. I was alone on a mountain canopied by soaring trees and an impermeable silence. Although the birds were chirping, everything else was undeniably still. A gush of wind made my blood freeze and compelled me to stretch the animal skin I was wearing to cover as much of my flesh as I could. As my feet stepped away from the dampness to escape into the inadequate warmth of dryness, they instead fell over a patch of ice that bit through the cracks in my sole. I had no recollection of why I was wandering thirsty, hungry and vanquished in some bewitched land blanketed by a soundless fear. I was lost and yet in my heart, there was an unmistakable longing for something.

With each step, the emotions of fear, curiosity and most of all, a yearning were taking a strong grip on my heartbeat and seemed to make it slower. Was I looking for something...or maybe it was someone? I didn't know if I could find anything to eat or drink but that didn't have any bearing on my instinct to go on. I placed my hand on the dagger tied to my waist, just to reassure myself of its presence. Hearing a low sound from a particular direction, I impulsively yet cautiously moved towards its source.

On getting closer, the sound became louder and more vibrant. It was perhaps music of some kind. The melody was becoming incessantly vivid and recognizable. The sound of the classical musical instruments unveiled a powerful, erotic and yet very serene rhythm. The music drew me towards its source, making me forget my fears. I marched forward to discover the origin of this divine descent. After a few steps, I saw an opening between the stems of two humongous trees. A dim light from the other side made its way revealing a narrow pathway. I followed its lead into the oblivion in one swift leap.

A cold breeze blew right through my skin. I sought the warmth of the magnificent lantern lit right next to the most beautiful Natraj Statue placed in a natural fissure in the rocks. On the ground, frost shimmered in the golden light, as if teasing the enormously dark open sky. Impassive to her surroundings, enamored with poise, I saw the silhouette of her dancing. Curious for a closer look, I tiptoed a little further with my breath getting heavier. I was entering uninvited into a strange territory. She was unbelievably beautiful, dressed like a goddess, dancing in ferocious movements. I dared not go too close, for I didn't want her to register my presence. I could see her but to her, I was like a shadow in the dark.

Her arms moved to create exquisite postures as the beats became intense. Even from afar, her eyes looked drunk on fire and the arch of her body kissed the threshold of liberty, as she danced her inhibitions away. She swayed with the wind, wild and free.

Her fingers opened like a flower with her elbows making a swift yet soft movement, in perfect rhythm with her feet. She was redeeming herself from her own clutches; her feet hitting the ground in a rebellious cry, as if lamenting all that she was denied. She was rejoicing her triumph over everything that pulled her down, with her waist jerking outward vivaciously. There seemed to be no stopping her tempestuous gale.

I was immobilized in my spot, for this experience was surreal and she was indeed enchanting. In abandon of my physical existence, I felt as if I was in heaven witnessing a cosmic dance by the divine feminine herself. Suddenly, the music stopped, and her feet stopped too. I lurched back into awareness of my surroundings in the immaculate silence that revealed everything. Shamefully, I looked away at being exposed. She stepped towards me, her *ghungroo* pronouncing her movement before her feet touched the ground. Knowing there was no escape, I found her close, looking at me right in my face.

Her eyes were still as ice, passionate as fire, moist as love, angry as Kali and as compassionate as Shiva. I could see her clearly now. She shut her eyes. Her face close enough for me to feel the warmth of her panting breath. Tears rolled down her eyes. Mustering my might, I stretched my hand to caress her cheek. Just when I touched her glowing skin, it was engulfed in a burst of flames. In a moment, she turned into ashes and fell on my feet.

"Maaya!" I screamed with my heart pounding heavily,

suddenly sitting bolt upright, scared awake from my dream. It was dreadful. My eyes were moist. Maaya had melted like a statue of wax right in my arms, turning into dust on my feet. A sword of fire seared through my body, giving me a sinking feeling that travelled down from my heart to my legs, making me weak and jittery.

"Are you okay?" Neha touched my hands wondering why I was sweating profusely, looking all flustered. I was sitting with eyes wide open on my bed at 2 a.m. It was her touch that pulled me out of that appalling momentum. I had disturbed her sleep. "I am fine. Thank you." I said, still feeling displaced and restless, pulling myself away from her hand.

She switched on the bedside lamp, looking at me intently. There was disappointment in her eyes. "When will you get over Maaya? She has been between us forever. I wonder why you chose to be with me if this was the level of attachment you had with her. Rahul, I think you should go and visit a shrink. You need help. I don't know what happened between the two of you, but I think you need to sort yourself out. This is not healthy. Not for you, neither for me nor for Anushkha. You must get over Maaya. She's long gone, Rahul!"

I was listening to her, though my mind was still pre-occupied with the dream. It was disgusting that I was unable to hide my despicable state from my wife. Neha was aware of how my inability to accept the loss of my ex was eating into the stability of my mind. Feeling even more exhausted, I curled up turning to the other side and closed my eyes.

Before losing myself to slumber, I couldn't help noticing my absolute inability to let go of Maaya. It was ridiculous to realize that while I was responsible for walking out on her, even hurting her to no end, I was still the one unconsciously holding on to her like a dying man holding on to his last breath.

As days and weeks passed, my life increasingly felt meaningless and purposeless. I often compared Neha to Maaya and blamed myself for having made the wrong choice. Neha was nothing of what I wanted, and Maaya was perhaps more than what I deserved. What I shared with Maaya couldn't be experienced again with anyone else, ever! I witnessed my incessant obsession over Maaya which was neither helping Neha nor my daughter. Everyone was suffering, and it was all on me.

One evening, after work, I wanted to have coffee alone. I had to introspect. There was hardly any place where I could be by myself. The Café next to my office building was my favorite hangout. Its classic wooden interiors and beige leather furniture gave me a cozy and comfortable experience. The aroma of freshly brewed coffee tantalized me and allowed me to slip into a warm comfortable space within myself. Stepping out of my office, I headed straight to the café.

Looking out of my window, sitting atop my high stool, I reminisced the times when I frequented his place with Maaya. I couldn't help regretting that I didn't know where Maaya was. She had given up her job long back and moved elsewhere. It had been over two years. She left no trail. It was fair, I told myself. I deserved it as I had hurt her too many times. In my own defense, I realized that the cost I was paying for sticking to my morals was weighing me down. I couldn't breathe, be happy or even participate in my own life.

Sipping my coffee, intoxicated by the bittersweet aroma of dark caramel, I decided to look for Maaya. I had been suppressing this thought under the heavy weight of my righteousness for quite some time, but no more. My choices weren't working for me, so I had to look for Maaya.

□

The Quest

"Anushkha please spare the laptop now. I have some important office work to do," saying which I lifted my 7-year-old daughter off her seat, plonking her on the floor. All this while, I had arrogantly distanced myself from social media asserting it to be an absolute waste of time. Now, however, I was desperate.

I opened my browser to logon to Friendsbook. I recalled Maaya mentioning having a profile on it. After quickly registering, I keyed her name in the search box and pressed Enter, waiting with bated breath for her beautiful face to light up my screen. My pulse was racing like a freight train. Unfortunately, a long list of pictures popped up with the same name and all sorts of different surnames. That didn't deter my quest. I patiently clicked on each profile picture to identify my lease of life. Finally, my eyes fell on an old picture of Maaya and hastily, I clicked on it. Her profile opened. My heart was galloping like a stallion on a racecourse. Not having been in touch with her all this while, I was yearning to know her whereabouts and perhaps see a few of her latest pictures.

For the next 20 minutes, I scrolled through every

single update on her timeline that was publicly visible. Regrettably, it gave me no clue about her whereabouts. She had last updated her status around the same time that we parted ways. I was disheartened. How else could I have reacted? Maybe this time, I had indeed lost her forever. A familiar sinking feeling returned. The void within me was haunting me like never before.

"Maaya, where are you?" I stomped my hand on my wooden study table, feeling exasperated. Anushkha got frightened. She started crying and ran to her mother who was cooking in the kitchen. I slammed shut the top of my laptop and lay down on my bed, blankly looking at the ceiling fan, feeling lost and gloomy.

Neha and I had frequent clashes and it were evident that we were incompatible. I was lost in the labyrinths of my thoughts, seeing no respite going forward. It felt like a cursed existence which was wretchedly filled with a growing recognition that I was solely responsible for making myself so despondent. I sometimes pitied myself and at other times I pitied Anushkha for the imperfect life I had created for her.

My arrogance had led me to where only Maaya could help me. She knew me better than myself. She could help me this one more time. Just then, a voice in my head whispered, "Isn't that selfish?"

I put tonnes of boulders over the unrest created within, for I couldn't afford it right now. I couldn't afford to be 'selfish' or 'undeserving' right now.

My quest led me to Maaya's old office. I presumed that at least Gagan, her ex-boss would certainly know about her coordinates. Seeking help from Gagan wasn't exactly appealing, though I knew I couldn't afford my ego either. I was determined to find Maaya, even if it was at the cost of being ridiculed.

"Hello, Dev," I greeted him. We were in the lift together. Upon a glance, he looked away feigning nonchalance. He blamed me for whatever Maaya endured. My guilt resurfaced. I wanted to comfort him, but I knew he wouldn't pay me any heed, so I just lowered my head down and waited for us step out. The lift stopped at the 5th floor. He calmly strode towards his cabin, completely ignoring me. I followed him till the reception where a sober looking lady was busy attending a call. I waited for her to acknowledge me.

"How can I help you sir?" she enquired in a polite tone. She was new, I thought, since the previous receptionist knew me by face. It wasn't surprising since, I had walked into that office after over two years.

"Hello! I would like to meet Gagan," I informed her.

"Do you have an appointment with him, Sir?" she queried.

"No, I don't but I really need to see him, please! It's personal and it's urgent," I found myself pressing on her.

"Sure Sir. Gagan Sir hasn't arrived yet. As soon as he arrives, I will inform him. May I please have your name Sir?" she smiled.

"Rahul Singhania."

I was requested to wait in their guest lounge. She was generous enough to order a café latte for me. The vibrant colors liberally used on the walls, with the abstract patterns transpiring in momentous ways, revealing different shades of life intrigued me. Advertising agencies and lifestyle magazines had the most imaginative and plush offices, for they were frequented by their clients on a regular basis. Their class had to be reflected well in their staff as well as office décor.

The sofa I was sitting on was elaborate and comfortable, with a few magazines lying on the table. I impatiently turned pages of the latest editions of their monthly magazine, ingenuously looked for Maaya's name on the columns but in vain.

"Hey Rahul!" I heard my name, just as I bent forward to keep the empty coffee mug on the table in front of me. Gagan was approaching me, with his hands stretched out for a handshake. I was relieved that Gagan hadn't refused to see me. He didn't look upset with me, unlike Dev.

"Come, let's go to my cabin," saying which he walked ahead expecting me to follow his lead. I abided.

I took up a seat opposite to him on the other side of his table, in his chic cabin.

"What's up bro? You don't look too great." he asked me, sounding concerned. "Yes, I am not doing too well Gagan. Where is Maaya, Gagan? Please tell me." I asked him straightaway.

For a moment he was silent. Then he straightened the back of his lazy chair and retorted, "Why do you want to know Rahul? I thought it was over between the two of you?"

The look in his eyes had changed. He was now cold and distant. "I hurt her Gagan, its true. I became a source of her pain. I regret it. I have tried hard to forget her, but it doesn't seem like a possibility. I think about her, dream about her and sometimes even hallucinate about her. I am slowly going crazy. In my misplaced entitlement, I only gave her passive aggressive rage, punishing her by being withdrawn and self-absorbed. My shame for having lost her is making me a vexed person. I fight with almost everyone these days. I am spiraling in the traps of my own mind, beleaguered with no respite. I can't sleep Gagan. Sometimes, I can't breathe. I want to ask her for forgiveness, Gagan. I must. I don't know how to move on in my life," I pleaded at the cost of sounding desperate.

I watched him transfixed, waiting to see if he would speak.

"Hmmmm. Isn't that a little selfish, Rahul?" he said looking at me as if he was searching for the answer not in my response but in my eyes.

"Why would you say so?" I asked in amazement.

"To be loved solely for her strengths was a torment. In her struggle to be strong, in her endeavor to be what you admired, she felt isolated. She was locked behind a mask, hiding behind it, her benevolent self. Yet finally, what broke her was your need to feel superior. You wanted to control her role in your life. The deformed ego you cradle as "self" permitted her to be the "wind beneath your wings" and not the bird soaring freely in the sky. You destroyed the person who loved you. She was your power and not your weakness. You never gave her credit for being your invisible spine, the one you relied on for support. She did the right thing by choosing herself over you. Crippled minds seldom become enablers. You don't get to choose to step back and forth in her life anymore, Rahul.

Each time you pursue her, it's not for her, neither is it for love. It's to relinquish yourself from your unbearable guilt, loneliness and gloom. The pretext is different, but you still 'need' her and don't 'love' her. Do you realize each time you entered her life, you brought hope but inevitably pushing her into a deep dark abyss of loneliness and rejection when you left? She has been vanquished, dishonored, betrayed and abandoned more often than she deserved.

The only way for her to protect her soul from getting scarred was to leave. If you warm her heart again, it might destroy her. For her sake and for the love you once promised her, you must let her go. You can't be unburdened of your shame now. You must live with it. You must see it on your face each day when you look at yourself in the mirror. It must compel you to change your way of being. You cannot escape the consequences of your choices on this plane. It doesn't work that way my friend. This time it is for you to find forgiveness on your own. She isn't here. She's moved on in her experience, leaving you to face your demons. You are on your own," he said, retreating from me.

I felt crushed but I knew he was right.

"Thanks, Gagan. Appreciate your candid response. Perhaps it's time. I must resolve my conflicts myself," I said as I shook hands with him and left his office.

I felt very lost the whole day and I skipped office too. It was a shame that each door that could have led me to her was shut on me. I didn't know where to look for her. Perhaps I wasn't meant to. Maybe Gagan was right. I had to take the reins of my life in my own hands.

My secretary called me a few times, but I couldn't be

bothered. I wanted to be by myself. Neha called but I just sent her a message saying I was busy. I drove on NH8 endlessly with no clue of where I was headed. I just knew I had to keep going. There was too much noise in my head. What Gagan had said pinched me. I had never thought about how Maaya would have dealt with her pain. She had always been so graceful. She always concealed her wounds but did the right thing. If she wanted, she could have objected to me allowing Neha to come and stay with me the first time around. I would have done whatever she expected of me, but she instead stepped back. She allowed me space to make my way to her by choice, at my own pace. Naïvely, she trusted me every time I told her that I wanted to be with her again.

ME TO HER

Whenever I wanted her,

She let me in,

Then slowly but lovingly,

She healed my wounds,

She wiped my tears and my fears,

With the warm touch of her soul,

She made me feel dear,

When I was strong and could roar,

Just when I was free to hold her back,

I moved on...as if she never was!

This was a poem that I had once read in a book and it resonated with how I had treated Maaya. My pain was only growing. My heart was aching. My tears wouldn't stop flowing. I wiped my tears only to ensure that I could see the road I was driving on. I didn't know how far I had come. It seemed to be late afternoon. I looked at my watch to realize it was 2 p.m. Seeing a signboard of "Cafe Coffee Shop" on my left, I pulled over. I was hungry and lost. A coffee could help.

The café had a very scruffy look. There was only one guy at the counter and no customers. I walked up to the counter and asked him to make me a Cafe Latte toned down with half shot. He agreed and requested me to be seated on the black leather sofa that looked as lonely and desolate as me.

"Where does this road lead to?" I asked him. He quizzically looked at me, saying "30 kms to Ajmer, Sir!" and got busy making my coffee. Astoundingly, I couldn't place Ajmer in my head for the first few seconds. I must have driven almost 200 kms without stopping anywhere. Since it was so close by, it only made sense that I should visit Ajmer Sharif. Ajmer Sharif is one of the most sacred "dargah" or Sufi shrine of the revered Saint Moinuddin Chishti. I had always felt drawn to it. I was secretly hoping for some peace by going to the sacred place. As my wandering eyes fell on the food counter, I also realized that I had forgotten to order something to eat. The Cheese sandwich seemed like the most appetizing choice. I ordered for it along with my coffee. Both were served to me together, soon. Just then, a longing to reach the shrine, a calling for something I didn't quite understand seemed to have been triggered within me in haste.

As soon as I finished eating, I thanked the barista and the next moment, I was headed towards Ajmer. The food and coffee seemed to have rejuvenated me. I felt more aware of my surroundings while driving towards the shrine.

Soon, I reached the city. I went across little gullies till I reached the "Buland Darwaza" and after depositing my shoes at a counter just outside, the first thing I noticed were a few shops on the left. I decided to buy a "chaddar," a colored sheet of cloth to be offered in prayer at the shrine. I bought the entire set of the prayer material offered.

Fortunately, a kind man saw me confused about where to head next and offered to guide me. He seemed like a maulvi and the place looked huge. His appearance was a blessing. He guided me to a rack of scarves and suggested that I first cover my head. Most religious places traditionally recommend entering the premises with a covered head. I chose a yellow colored scarf and tied it neatly on my head.

He then guided me inside the dargah. There were many people lined up in a queue before me, but my guide seemed to be an influential person. He managed to get me in earlier than many others in the queue. I simply followed him. Inside the big room where the sepulcher was placed, they covered my head with my sheet. I had to pray to "Khwaja Saheb" from beneath it. As I was about to close my eyes, I saw Maaya standing with me. She looked at me in the eye and just when I was about to touch her face, the sheet was pulled off my head and my guide asked me to move since there were other people waiting for their turn. I was a little zapped at what had just happened. I ached for that moment to return. I wanted to touch her. I wanted to talk to her. I wanted to cry burying my head in her chest, but she was gone.

We were soon out of the shrine in the open area. I noticed two women standing in the middle of the ground randomly shaking their head in round circles, with their hair swinging so vigorously that it looked scary. I asked my guide why they were doing this. Before he could answer, a man came near one of the women and started hitting her with a broom. She screamed yet made no attempt to save herself. Her position was stationary. She didn't even care to see who was beating her on the back. It was preposterous. Everyone around was going about their normal business. No one was bothered about the screaming woman. I was astonished. My guide sensed my anxiety, and as I turned around to enquire from him, he bent closer and whispered "Sir, these women are possessed by disembodied spirits. These spirits have total control of their body. They have been brought to this holy place so that they can be freed. When they are being hit, it's the spirit who has possessed them that gets affected. It will force it to leave them alone. They will be fine in just a few minutes. There are many who find their release to the light with the blessings of our revered saint!" he said with a tinge of pride in his tone.

Esotericism was not my comfort zone. My analytical mind did not let me accept what it did not understand. I was pre-occupied, so I quietly moved into a secluded corner where I could avoid the view. This man had guided me well, so I offered him some money which he gladly accepted. With folded hands I expressed my gratitude and sat cross legged to introspect and pray privately in my chosen place. He left.

As I closed my eyes, the enormous noise in my head returned. Even after sitting in meditation for a while, there was extreme restlessness, anxiety and a feeling of being lost. I had heard that high energy places like this shrine usually had a magical impact on people, where they find peace within; nothing of the sort happened with me. I was still struggling with the zillions of thoughts that clouded my thinking. Just then, while I was tangled in my choice for the next step, a hand gently sat on my head. I opened my eyes. A very graceful tall elderly man wearing an Arabic kind of outfit with a headgear was looking at me straight in my eyes. "What bothers you so much child?" he asked me.

"I am confused about my life decisions baba. I have hurt someone who has loved me a lot. I can't seem to move on from her. I can't forgive myself, nor can I forget her," I said.

"You can't hurt someone who loves you child, for love never wanted anything from you. It is not the nature of love to take. It only comes to give and disappears one day when your vessel is too full to receive its benevolent blessings," he said.

It took me a moment to grasp the depth of what he had said. I realized it was true. Realizing that she didn't want anything from me, I felt even guiltier of hurting her.

"What if I have kept her under false hope? What if she always deserved someone better than me? What if I held on to her knowing that I didn't have the courage to offer her the kind of life she deserved?"

"Do you have that courage now son?" he asked me

I was slightly taken aback by his question. I wasn't

prepared for it. I didn't know the answer.

"I don't know yet baba."

"Then find that first. Without understanding yourself if you seek her again, you will end up repeating everything you regret. You must understand her purpose in your life. To be able to give her love, you must have it within. You are yet to find it for yourself. That's where you should be headed." he said

"Can I be with her in this lifetime? Can you help me know what I want?" I asked him like a child wanting to be told what to do next.

"The day your love for her will cease to look for her in form or in a way that you want, that day, you will experience a reunion and you will be united with her forever!"

I was instantly sad. To me it meant that I couldn't be with her.

"This choice doesn't lie with me or God Rahul. It lies with you."

I lowered my head with shame and disappointment.

Just then, I raised my head to ask the wise man another question, but he had vanished. Panicking, I got up and searched for him but couldn't find him anywhere around. Maybe he thought the conversation was over and thus he left.

Surprisingly, I felt lighter and a bit relieved after talking to him. I started to remind myself of what he advised, to understand what my next step should be. While I was still contemplating, there was a boy who came selling some souvenirs of the shrine. There were some symbols made of metal, some beaded strings and to my surprise, there was a picture. He was holding it very close to his heart and it didn't look like he intended to sell it. It attracted me. I asked him to show it to me up close. With a very guarded look, he carefully handed over the framed picture and said, "Khwaja Saheb!" There was an unmistakable hint of pride in his voice.

When I saw the picture, I was dumbfounded. It was the picture of the same old wise man who was talking to me just a few minutes ago. I didn't quite understand it when he said "Khwaja Saheb" or maybe I didn't believe it, so I asked, "How can I meet him?"

He anxiously took the picture from my hands, as if he was feeling offended and responded, "In our hearts, he will live till eternity but in this realm, he left us 800 years ago!"

That is when it sunk in. I couldn't believe this boy. I couldn't believe myself either. I had just spoken to this man. He was here with me and had answered my questions. The man was "Saint Moinuddin Chishti." How could this be? It is then that I recalled that he addressed me with my name, though I had not shared it with him. This realization made me even more anxious, for I felt I was becoming a lunatic.

I was bewildered, not knowing how to fathom what had just occurred with me. I left the place instantly to allow myself some time to absorb what has just transpired. It was almost sunset, and I had been tirelessly driving for most part of the day. It was best to stay in a motel on the highway and perhaps go home the next day.

Soon, I checked in to the nearest decent place I could find. I couldn't be bothered with verifying the rating of the property as long as it had a nice, clean room I could rest in. I was readily offered a room and in just a few minutes, I was in the lap of a cozy white bed, looking at the artistically done ceiling and wondering about my life.

It was the longest night. I gazed at the still fan all night with a sense of bareness in my heart. When I checked the time, it was 4 a.m. My attention went to several missed calls including a few from Neha too. I disinterestedly sent her a message, mentioning that I was fine and would be home by the next evening.

My body was aching and from every bone in my body, I wanted to just hibernate and never go back home. I was exhausted with my inner conflict and nothing made sense to me. I didn't even know what made me feel so lost and miserable. The latent sanity in me reminded me that I couldn't afford to miss work for yet another day. Post sunrise, I went to my car to take out the spare business suit which I always had in my car for emergency meetings. Within 20 minutes, I had freshened up, eaten the banana placed in my room with a black coffee and was driving towards my office.

As I tuned into FM, my favorite old Hindi song was playing. My mood changed, and I started feeling a bit lighter. Maybe the previous day's events and my visit to the shrine helped shed some light on my inner darkness. The cheerful song also contributed.

The following week, I felt calmer during the days, but evenings were becoming heavy and lonely. I was relentlessly searching for Maaya at the back of my mind. Dunking myself in work was becoming my way of staying sane. I didn't want to slip into depression. By the time I reached back home,

Anushkha was almost asleep. Neha and I hardly ever talked. I either ate at the office canteen or picked a sandwich on my way home. It was a strange feeling coming back home. I met my girl very briefly on weekends because either I was working over the weekends, or she had gone for her dance or art classes. I felt sad for her and perhaps even pitied her but that's as much as I could manage. Those days I pitied myself more than anyone. There was no scope to take on more guilt or compensate for relationships I could see I wasn't actively being a part of. At times Neha bugged me with unnecessary questions about my whereabouts and at other times I felt sad for giving her a life so deprived of love and companionship. I felt conflicted and chaotic within. I could do no more. I could only just let each day pass with everything that seemed conflicting, both externally and internally. I was hoping for some heavenly miracle to sort out what I had created.

□

Divine Intervention

I wasn't performing as per the expectations of my line management. My appraisal was due in a couple of weeks. My mind was constantly preoccupied with an oblivious quest. I had to make up for a lot, even at my workspace. I consciously resolved to focus wholly on my work for some time. It could help me save my high paying job. Becoming more mechanical and denying emotions seemed to be the only way. I knew distractions didn't work in the long run, but to ensure survival, whatever worked was fine.

Taking breaks only for meals, constantly pushing caffeine into my system and recklessly working round the clock was my new mantra. My performance rallied. After putting three weeks of hard labor, we saw the addition of two more clients on board, which washed away all my previous sins. If one could bring business to a corporate, they became the privileged ones overnight. I was amazed that in my most debilitated mental state, I could still rope them into the financial bid. I had to give myself this one. My sanity otherwise those days seemed to be borrowed. Days were still bearable but at night, darkness pressed in and I felt hollow within. I would curl up and then toss from one side to another in the hope of getting some sleep, but it would mostly elude me until the wee hours. In that dark bareness, life seemed so futile. I used to wake in the night, wishing for the sun. Slowly, my face started looking weary with puffiness under my eyes. I was losing interest in communicating with others, in eating, in going out, in life overall. I was beginning to lose weight drastically. Finally, I accepted that I had to see a shrink.

It was odd for an egoist like me to accept that I needed help to understand my own mind, but I could deny it no further. I was burning myself out at work and nothing seemed to make me happy. With the recommendation from a friend at work, I took an appointment with a good doctor for the following week.

The appointment was on a Monday morning. I was nervous as I had never done this before. The clinic seemed welcoming and had a chic reception where I was asked to wait before the doctor could call me. I was given a form to fill with my basic details. In another 10 minutes, it was my turn. The first glimpse of the doctor was a surprise and a relief. I was expecting this old spectacled lady sitting on a big armchair looking down at me from beyond her specs placed on her nose, scrutinizing each move of mine as I settled in my chair. However, here instead was a charming young lady who greeted me with a smile as she offered me a seat.

She asked me to share what compelled me to visit her. I told her a few things about whatever I had been going through, including a brief history of my relationship with Maaya. Somehow, while sitting in her cabin, I felt she wouldn't be able to help me. She asked me many questions and even prescribed some pills. Thanking her, I walked out. Something didn't quite click. I didn't feel completely convinced about it being the right way to know myself from within. I had an inkling as if I was seeking something else. I decided not to carry on with my visits to her, going forward.

"It's so tough! I am stuck. I don't know what I want. I don't know if this is what I chose. I want to run away and yet I don't know if I can. Dear lord, please help me. If there are any angels, any divine beings that exist, please show me the way," I prayed in my head. My experience at Ajmer Sharif and my compelling circumstances were turning me into a believer.

Maaya used to tell me about angels and divine beings but I was on my own at the time. I didn't pay much attention to most of other worldly conversations that we had. To me, it was perhaps what she found solace in, even if they were mere stories she created in her head. There was no point regretting anymore. I had to move forward and find a way to break free from my self-imposed crutches. I was too obsessed with my regrets and they didn't let me sleep or relax.

It was already 11 p.m. and I had a long day ahead, so I reluctantly decided to rest. I was tired and luckily, I was able to sleep by mid-night.

I woke up with a tremble. I heard something. It was still dark outside my window. It wasn't possible that someone could knock on my bedroom door. The house was locked from inside and there wasn't anyone else except me at home. Neha and my daughter were away at her parents' place. I gave the thought a pass. Perhaps I was just imagining it. I went back to sleep.

In a few seconds, I heard a knock. Could it possibly be someone? Distressed, I looked around. There was nobody near me. I checked the time in the dim light of the night bulb. It was exactly 2:00 a.m. I asked a few times for who was there. Again, someone knocked the door. In fear, concern and suspicion, I opened my bedroom door partially. As I raised my phone torch to see who it was, I was shocked. A very divine elderly man dressed in a white robe standing, eluding white light was standing at my door with a lamp in his hand. He seemed charismatic only by the look of it. "It's God himself," I found myself thinking while opening the door fully.

I was too stunned to say any more than, "*who are you?*" in a soft mild tone.

"I am Michael. I came here to help you. You summoned me here."

"I summoned you. Really" I said, still wondering when and how I could have called him. Before I could say anything, he spoke again.

"You asked the lord for help, so here I am. I am an angel. I was sent to guide you. Tell me what you wish to understand?"

"Angel Michael," oh yes, I realized. I knew this name. Maaya had mentioned him so many times. He was for real. A tinge of shame and excitement ran down my spine.

He maintained a calm and compassionate posture. There was so much love in his eyes. I felt as if he had already forgiven me for being so naïve.

"Please help me Angel Michael. I don't know what's happening to me. I don't even know myself anymore. Ever since Maaya has gone, I don't seem to like my life anymore. I know I have hurt her, but I want her back. She knew me so well. She loved me, cared for me and never asked for anything in return. I miss her love. I want to make it up to her dear angel. Please tell me what I should do?"

"Hmmmm. So, you want her back so that she can love you. Right?"

"Yes and of course I would love her back too."

"Do you understand what love is, Rahul?" asked Michael

"Perhaps I do or perhaps I don't. I may not know much about love, but I have realized that I can't live without her."

"Rahul, do you remember that red Ferrari toy car you used to have when you were seven years old?" said Michael

"Yes, I do. How do you know about it?"

"I know a lot more than what you'd imagine. Do you remember how you kept howling and crying for two days before your school exams for that car? You told your parents that you would write your exams only if they would buy it for you."

My head stooped towards the ground. "Yes, Angel Michael. I remember!"

"Do you know where that car is now?" he asked

"No Angel. I don't know. I lost interest in it after I grew up. It was one of my favorites though."

"Exactly! Maaya is like that car for you. You want her

now because you miss her, but you don't understand why. You don't know anything about the void in yourself that she fills."

"No Angel Michael, I love her. I will never let her go this time."

"Rahul, where is the place for her in your life? Think about it. Your life is too full."

I suddenly realized he was talking about my family. He was right. I had not yet created a place for Maaya. How could she stay with me? Before I could say another word, he spoke again.

"I am not talking about your wife and your child. You don't have space for them either. You don't have space for love within yourself. By living with someone, you don't necessarily give them what they want. Your family is equally miserable because they don't feel your love. You are not giving anyone anything."

Those words tore me apart. He was right. I only believed I was doing my best to keep everyone happy, but I never saw their misery in all of this.

As I looked up at the angel again, a bright light sparkled luminously in my face and I found myself rubbing my eyes in my bed. It was morning and our help had just drawn the window curtains on the left side of my bed. That's how she had been instructed to wake me up in case I was found sleeping beyond bedtime. She had an extra pair of keys to unlock the apartment. I was a little shocked as well as surprised. It was already 8 a.m. Was he real? Did all of it happen? Was I dreaming? I wasn't sure. I couldn't afford to spend any more time in bed, no matter how much I would have liked to go over the entire scene with Angel Michael in my head.

There was a certain heaviness in my head the entire day. I was working but some part of my mind seemed to be off. I was in awe of my most recent encounter with the mystical world. It was uncanny. I was compelled to think if I was, in fact being watched over.

Once I reached home, I finished my dinner early and went to sleep.

"What should I do? Where should I go? I don't know where she could be. I wish I would have asked the angel," these were the thoughts which woke me up at dawn, as if in panic.

Just then it clicked... Singapore!

She had once told me that if she ever wanted to forever abandon me and hide, she would settle down in Singapore. She loved the city and its people so much. It was like second home to her. I wondered if she had indeed moved there.

I was still contemplating what my next step should be, when serendipity happened, at its best. Just three days later, my boss suggested my name for an assignment in Singapore. I was taken aback at the speed at which my thoughts were manifesting into the real world. It was surreal.

The approval came through. I chose Singapore though the opportunity came exactly when I could also choose to go to Hawaii, which was my dream destination. My gut feeling told me that I should go to Singapore. I couldn't believe I was insane enough to pack my bags and go to a new country just to look for Maaya, knowing well enough that in the bleak chance that I could find her, she wouldn't want to see my face.

It was okay, I told myself. I just had to see her once. I just had to tell her how all that she ever tried to show me, I was seeing now. I just had to tell her how she was the most precious part of me that I lost. What a big fool I had been. I accepted the assignment. Just when I was packing my bags, my little girl came up to me. "Papa, why are you going to Singapore alone? I want to come with you." Somewhere in my heart, the thought of leaving her made me feel torn.

Was I to tell her that I was going to look for Maaya? Was I ready to tell her that I didn't intend to spend the rest of my life with her mother?

I didn't know my answers. I didn't know what I was doing. This time I just had to progress. I was unaware of my destination, but I had to take the next step. It was not a choice my mind would have allowed me, but the signs were coercing me for once, to flow with my heart. I didn't know why I wanted to see her and what I would say if I did see her. I didn't want to think of all this just yet. For now, I just wanted to believe in the possibility of getting one more chance to make it up to her.

"You can't come with me to where I am going sweetheart." I said to Anushkha as I lifted her off my lap. She had been pleading me to take her along to Singapore. "I am sorry, but I am in this alone," I said as I resumed my packing. She was confused with my reply, so she quickly ran up to her mother to ask her if she could travel with me.

Upon packing my bags, without engaging in much conversation, I bid goodbye to Neha and Anushkha. I couldn't look into my wife's eyes for I feared she would know. I gave a peck on the cheek of my daughter, asked them to take care of themselves and left without looking back even once. I didn't want to change my mind. I wanted to just leave.

□

In La La Land

"Is the air conditioning working?" I asked the air hostess.

"Yes sir. Do you want me to lower the temperature a bit? Will that be more comfortable?" she asked being most polite.

I pulled my tie down my neck, breathing better. "Yes, that would be kind of you."

"Certainly sir," she responded before moving towards the front arch with a smile.

"Hey!" I called out to her again, just in case she'd come back.

"Yes sir. Is there anything else I can help you with?" she returned to my seat.

"Could you pour me a gin and tonic please?" I requested.

"Certainly sir. As soon as the plane takes off, I'll bring your drink. Would that be fine sir?" she enquired.

"Sure. Thank you"

My brain was fogged. Giving it much thought was perilous. I had once read that life's most beautiful experiences happened when one stepped into the unknown. The known is too predictable to create miracles. This decision to go Singapore was the most bizarre thing I had ever done in my life. I was nervous, yet excited.

As I drew a deep breath making myself comfortable in my recliner seat, it all started feeling better. Thanks to the perks of working for one of the biggest consulting firms, I always flew first class. It certainly made the journey a wee bit easier. I indulged myself in the movies and wine throughout the flight. Sleep eluded me, so indulging in the little pleasures of life was my way of recuperating a bit and getting ready for the days to come. I hardly knew what awaited me next.

This was my first trip to Singapore where I intended to stay any longer than the usual 2-3 days. This time I was thinking of staying there for much longer, maybe, till I found Maaya. My assignment was for a few months and I had the flexibility to extend it, provided they liked me. Something told me I would not be going back to India soon.

I took a cab from the Changi Airport and checked into my service apartment near the Raffles station in CBD. It was past 8 p.m. when I reached my apartment. At night, the city exuded a magnificence which is so evident while crossing the slender, shiny, well-lit skyscrapers and stupendously colored fountains in the middle of the business district.

My company had arranged my stay at one of the best serviced apartments with a rooftop swimming pool, two in-house restaurants, a 24 hours Starbucks opposite to it and a very well-equipped gym. As far as I was concerned, if the gym, an occasional swim, food and a good coffee were taken care of, I could easily feel at home. If material abundance could give me happiness, then this place had more than enough to offer. However, with the mental state that I was in, maybe nothing could really make me happy. Nevertheless, I was appreciative of my surroundings. They were uplifting and energizing to say the least.

I quickly settled down and asked the reception for the numbers of interesting order-in food joints. They gave me a few. I ordered pepperoni pizza and then unpacked my stuff. Then I took a quick shower to freshen up.

While looking for water I realized that my fridge was stocked with wine, beer and milk. The countertop had some stock of green tea, coffee, biscuits and some nuts. Of course, my secretary would have arranged it all. I pulled out a can of Heineken and split open a packet of roasted nuts. Just then the pizza delivery guy knocked at the door.

With my steaming hot pepperoni pizza and beer, I sat on the couch next to the window in my living room, which overlooked the city lights. It was an aesthetically done apartment with all facilities one could possibly imagine. It was comfortable, dimly lit and perfect to have a good time all by myself. However, as I watched the thousands of lighted homes, hotels, shops, cars and people, the vastness of it all triggered my inner restlessness again. I wondered where Maaya would be in the immensity I could see from my 18th floor apartment. I didn't even know if she had moved on with someone else. I didn't know how I would find her and when I did find her, what would happen then. It was all too chaotic and hence, not thinking too much was the best solution. I decided to sleep it off since it had been a long journey and I had been awake since early morning. Perhaps sleep was the best escape from my restlessness.

The next morning, I got ready, picked up a coffee and

sandwich from the Starbucks on my way and walked up to my client's office tracing my path with Google maps. I had been there before. It was a plush office in one of the tallest towers in Clark Quay. I was asked to wait at the reception while Johnny, my account manager came to receive me.

Johnny was a tall, bald and chubby white man. Judging from his accent, I was sure Johnny was from Europe. He greeted me warmly and invited me to his side of the floor. I was introduced to his team and then shown my cabin. This was where I had to spend most of my days, and maybe nights for the next few weeks while we listed their company on the Singapore Stock Exchange.

Luckily enough, though my office cabin was tiny, it had a wide window through which I could see the riverfront. It was a breath-taking view. Beautiful things outside often quickly triggered one's ugliness within. I was hoping the serenity of the view spared me my inner mess.

My next few days were busy. I plunged myself in work. My quest for Maaya began to slowly subside. The 24-hour Starbucks and McDonald's outlets across my apartment helped. I worked from home several times a week and a good coffee or burger helped me rejuvenate every few hours.

One evening I came home early, so I decided to cook myself a nice meal and enjoy it with some wine. This was one of those days when I had met a deadline and thus was in a rather good mood. As I rummaged through the fridge; there was nothing to cook. No vegetables. No cheese either. I quickly ran down to the seven eleven store and picked up some stuff. It was in the neighborhood. Within barely

20 minutes, I returned with some fresh greens, plenty of mushrooms, a can of coconut milk, rice cakes and some shrimps. I also bought some Laksa paste. There were some rice noodles lying in the cupboard, so I was all set to cook some authentic Singaporean Laksa. The first time I tasted Laksa was during a dinner meeting the previous week and it was fantastic. The moment I saw the Laksa paste at the supermarket, I decided to buy the necessary ingredients to enjoy Laksa for dinner in the quiet and serene atmosphere of my apartment, while watching the hustle bustle of the glitzy city.

The Australian Woodbridge white wine available at the supermarket was one of my favorite ones. The evening was all set with good wine followed by good food. I also managed to pick a packet of prawn crackers to nibble with my drink.

After a long time, I was feeling relaxed and pampered. The Laksa turned out well. Simply following the instructions given at the back of the pack was enough. Sipping wine in dim light, humming the old Hindi songs playing in the background was the perfect scene. I enjoyed myself thoroughly.

As I switched off the lights to call it a day, my phone beeped. I ignored it. It beeped again. "Who could this be?" I thought. No one really sent me messages on my Singapore number. Only my office colleagues had it and once I was off from work, there was no culture of disturbing anyone in their personal space unless it was an utmost necessity.

I reluctantly dragged myself to the dining table to pick my phone and check the messages. As I opened the first one, it said "Rahul, why are you in Singapore?"

This was Maaya. I was sure, it was her. No one else dared to ask me about anything the way she could. The message was from a private number. I was excited, restless and fearful all at once. I didn't know what to do. I wanted to call her, talk to her and ask her how she was. However, a private number cannot be called back. I could only reply to her message. However, what was I supposed to say? Should I have told her that I came here looking for her? Should I have said instead that an office assignment brought me here? Would she be upset if I told her that I was chasing her, or would she be upset if I told her that my visit to Singapore was a coincidence which had nothing to do with her?

I was confused. I didn't know what to say. I didn't know the right answer. I just replied saying "Hi Maaya! Is this you?"

The phone was kept next to me all night. Every few minutes I checked if she wrote back but alas, she never did. I re-sent my message, but she chose not to respond. The ray of light was gone. I had lost her to the dark again. The only silver lining was that she knew I was in Singapore and she also had my number. She could reach me whenever she was ready. That was some solace. However, there was a slim chance that she would do anything of the sort. In fact, it was also possible that she would rather travel elsewhere whilst I was in Singapore to ensure we never met. I knew her too well. She was the most righteous woman. Her knowledge of me being in Singapore could do more harm than good to us. However, I had no control over it now. She already knew. I didn't even know how.

Maaya was on my mind all over again. Just when I had begun to accept my life in the lack of her presence, she seemed to have arrived right back in. I was perhaps guilty of forgetting her and enjoying Singapore for those few days that I did. I didn't deserve anything but continuous pain and regret, I reminded myself.

A few days later, Gagan got in touch with me on my Indian number. He informed me that he would be visiting Singapore for a meeting the coming week and if I was up for it, we could share a meal together. I was not sure why Gagan had any interest in meeting me, especially after our last conversation. Honestly, I was resistant to meeting him. He could look through me and I knew I lacked clarity about my stand for Maaya and her place in my life. It was possible that he would be able to see through my confusion. I didn't want that. However, perhaps he knew where she was and could give me a clue. I couldn't afford the chance to slip, hence I agreed.

Throughout the next day, I was extremely busy preparing a presentation for a new client. I reached home around 10 p.m. Just when I was ready to get some rest, my mind popped this uncomfortable question my way, "Why am I seeking Maaya? What will I say if I meet her? Am I ready to face her? Can I offer her anything? Have I sorted out my own life? Do I really want to sort it out?"

It was strange. Weren't these the same awkward questions that were thrown at me by Khawaja Saheb, Angel Michael and then Gagan? I became restless. I was hoping to buy more time. I didn't have the answers...at least not yet.

A terrible headache triggered. The best solution was to

take a medicine and go to sleep, and that's exactly what I did.

The next morning, I woke up feeling better.

"Hello papa, when are you coming back home?" asked Anushkha the moment I answered her call early in the morning. "Hello princess. How are you doing?" I replied.

"I am good papa, but I miss you."

"Aww. I will still take a few days Anushkha. My work here is not done yet. Do you want anything from here baby?"

"No papa. I want you to come back soon," she said.

"I miss you too darling. Will be back soon. Now I must get ready for work. Will call you later. Bye!" I said as I cut the line.

I instantly became sad. I couldn't continue talking to her, as it was painful to hear her innocent way of expressing her feelings for me.

I still lay in my bed, looking at the white ceiling. The blankness reminded me of the void in my heart. How could I run away from my daughter? How would I deal with my marriage? I wondered if my situation had any solution. I wondered if I had the courage to manifest a life of my choice.

Anushkha was only a little over 7 years and she needed me. She was my responsibility, and my separation from Neha would destroy an aspect of her life forever. Just then i thought of Aryan. Maaya had been so brave when she filed for her divorce. I recalled a conversation I had with her a few years back. "Maaya, don't you think you have been unfair to Aryan by separating him from his father?" I asked her. She looked at me with a penetrating look in her eyes. "I am not sure Rahul. I believe with the conflicts between me and Kunal, Aryan was bound to lose at least one parent. Perhaps that was a choice he had come with in this life. The more I lived in that marriage, the more lifeless I was becoming. I could have chosen to continue but in that case, Aryan would have lost his mother sooner or later. I could have stayed alive physically but my contribution and presence in his life would have been next to nil. I could have given him a normal parenting setup for namesake, but his experience would have been of grief, sadness and conflict. Instead I decided to give him and myself a chance by letting go of Kunal. His bond with Kunal can't be severed and it will exist nevertheless, however, by separating from him, I have made way for new hope to enter his life as well as mine. This way Aryan can have both parents, maybe not together but both, nevertheless. This choice might even teach Aryan that one who cannot save his own sanity cannot contribute to another's growth. Aryan and I are happy with the choice we made. He has a good relationship with his father as well as his mother. He lives life in awareness that it isn't perfect, yet he understands that perfection is a mirage and making the most of this moment is the best choice one can make. He is not growing up assuming all relationships work perfectly and hence he makes efforts to check his conduct with others and is sensitive to their needs. It has made him more aware and sensitive to his surroundings and he values love. He values people who stand by him. The maturity and kindness with which he conducts life, he has gained by accepting his life's truth" she said.

This conversation always inspired me to see why I should make that difficult choice not only for my sake but also for the sake of Anushkha's well-being. I was becoming emotionally and mentally unavailable to her. I was running away from her because I was pre-occupied with my inner conflicts. Moreover, it was difficult to face Neha. It was evidently not her fault, but neither was it mine. We just didn't belong together. I knew this for a long time now, yet I was holding on to my picture-perfect family. Besides, I was chasing Maaya and looking for her everywhere. I wondered if I was expecting Maaya to make a choice for me, again. Was Gagan right? Perhaps he was. I was indeed so dependent on Maaya...or perhaps I didn't want to take ownership of the path I would end up walking on? Or maybe I wanted her to choose my family for me, so that my guilt for her wouldn't follow me like a shadow for the rest of my life. But...I loved her too...or didn't I?

I was going mad. It was all so twisted in my head. "I am selfish. That's true. I hardly know what I want but I am holding on to everyone in my life, fearing I might need them later," I said to myself. I was then reminded of the incident I had at the Ajmer Sharif dargah where this is what baba told me. He told me that I must first clear my intent else I would end up recreating everything that I regret. He was right. I was already creating a loop back to where I started from.

After all this ruminating, I realized again that I needed professional help. This time instead of going to a shrink, I wanted to go to a holistic healer. I knew Maaya got a lot of help through her healing sessions to be able to deal with her inner turmoil. When she shared her experiences, I didn't completely believe them. By now I had realized that I had been a complete jerk who didn't pay attention to a lot of meaningful stuff. So much for ego, I thought. For me, seeking help was a sign of weakness. I didn't understand that it needed so much more courage to accept that one needed help.

The last few weeks had revealed to me my innermost fears and rigidity. It was time to open myself up to whatever I had resisted so far. I needed to break through the limitations of my mind. I needed a fresh perspective. I was so ready!

Maaya always said that if one's intent is clear; the universe conspires to help. I was now just going to walk the path of less mind and more faith. I couldn't go wrong. I got up from the bed with renewed energy.

I talked to a few colleagues at work, asking them of how I could get in touch with a good healer. They promised to come back to me with references. It was a good starting point. At least I was taking some initiative to address my conflicts.

□

Healing Cottage

I stepped into a wooden cottage built inside a small farm near the East Coast road. The address was right but there was no one in sight. The walkway led me to a reception, which was wooden brown with many wind chimes hanging from the ceiling. The walls were heavily decorated with antique pieces and the place had a very rustic feel to it. I had always expected a Healer's home to be as cozy as this house felt. Helen was referred to me by my Chinese friends and they reckoned she was very good. I waited till the house help showed up. She confirmed my name and guided me into a small room on the left. A young woman dressed in a bohemian outfit, wearing lots of beaded jewelry and a red headgear greeted me from across her table.

"Hello Mr. Rahul. Good to see you," she said shaking my hand as she greeted me. She offered me a seat across her on the opposite side of the table.

Her eyes, like an indigo colored ocean, were pools of iridescent blue, sculpted upon her creamy face like dazzling jewels. Strands of molten gold tumbled out of her scalp, cascading down her back like a waterfall. Cherry lips, crystal white teeth: she truly was a beautiful sight to behold.

Helen was indeed a beautiful Asian girl. With her intriguing eyes and petite frame, she seemed warm and pleasant. She had an air of wisdom, as if she knew more than most; not in an arrogant sort of way though. Some detachment perhaps, which seemed to connect her more with a higher consciousness was evident in her comportment. She adjusted her posture to sit up straight after closing the book she was reading.

"Mr. Rahul, I know we have had a brief email exchange about what brings you to me. However, I would greatly appreciate if you could share your story with me again now. It will help me connect with it better. It will also make it easier for me to understand my role in your journey. Even if it makes you uncomfortable, I would highly appreciate you do it, nevertheless. Let the discomfort surface," not really giving me a choice.

I shared with her my entire story relentlessly conveying both my escapism and my chase for Maaya with my inability to accept my wife and my marriage. She patiently heard me out without saying too much. She encouraged me to unburden myself and that's exactly what I did. For the first time I could say things that sounded strange to myself. A lot of revelations came out which, before that day I had never allowed myself to acknowledge. I needed to be honest in accepting all my inner conflicts, if I was truly seeking help. I wanted to do this by providing Helen with the complete picture, or at least my version of it. I was of course oblivious to many aspects which I was yet to discover during my journey. This was just the beginning.

When I finished talking, I realized an hour had already

passed. Helen noticed when I looked at my watch.

"Are you in a hurry?"

"No. I was just wondering if I had managed to consume all the time, I had with you in only talking about myself," I muttered. "That's ok. This will help. I don't time my sessions very stringently. I understand that we need to first understand the issue to be able to resolve it. In fact, an issue if correctly understood, itself starts presenting a solution. We have enough time. Leave that to me," she said. Upon listening to this, I felt relaxed. I anyway didn't like the idea of being rushed against the clock.

"Helen, do you think I am a very messed up person who has unrealistic expectations from life?"

"How messed up you are will be solely based on your perception of your conflicts. Expectations are unfortunately never realistic. Expectation itself means one wants life other than what is playing out through them. There is an evident disconnect between expectation and reality which then translates into various other emotions when one insists on living their expectation at the cost of their reality. Their entire life could start looking like one big lie."

I had never thought of expectations this way, but it made sense. She knew what she was talking about. Her perspective was unique. Her lack of judgement made me feel at ease. I could be open about my emotions.

"Let's do this Rahul," she said as she got up from her chair and pulled another chair closer to me and sat right across. She stretched out her hands as if asking for mine. Holding my hands in hers, she asked me to close my eyes and she did too. I felt a divine peace settling in as if her holding my hand was reassurance enough that all would be well.

I lost sense of time for a while. I can't recall if I was thinking something or if I blanked out, but I felt completely relaxed. Soon, I started to see a female figure sitting in some dark corner of a room and she was sobbing profusely. Her head was buried in her knees, and I couldn't see her face. She seemed to be very sad and broken. I could almost feel her pain in my chest. I started to get anxious. I wanted to pull my hand away from Helen and leave her place. Perhaps Helen sensed my resistance. She tightened her grip on my hand. Suddenly a sort of light passed through me and the vision disappeared. I started to feel calm again. The grief of that lady left a lasting impact on me. As if some untouched part of me had opened its door, beyond which was a carcass. I knew whatever was coming my way, I had to deal with it, yet, I was in denial. I tried to think it must have been something...but nothing to do with Maaya. It couldn't be her. No. It just couldn't be. I waited while Helen was still doing something with my energies. Her eyes were closed. I closed back mine too.

In a few minutes, Helen gave a deep sigh, withdrawing her hands from me. She told me I could open my eyes. There was deep sadness in her eyes. Perhaps...no I think I did...I saw a tear roll down her eyes. "What happened Helen?"

"Rahul, I saw a past life of yours and it was just too overwhelming. It wasn't my life but when I am connected with someone's energies, I can feel their deepest emotions in my body almost as mine," Helen said.

"Can you share with me about what you saw Helen?

I also saw something. It has left me feeling restless and anxious, but I first want to know what you got," I said hoping against hopes that she wouldn't say something that I didn't want to hear.

Helen pushed her chair a little away from me only to release the tension between her and me, so that she could share with me what she had experienced.

"Rahul, I saw a scene in which you were in an intimate position with a lady. It was a village setting and you were giggling with her in bed and both of you were completely immersed in love making."

She stopped, looked at me as if to gauge my reaction. Then she continued "Suddenly I saw that the room had a window with a horizontal iron grill on it. Both of you were unaware that the window was open. Another lady was standing outside the window, looking at both of you," she said. As Helen was narrating the story, my heart started pumping faster. I knew this wasn't going right.

"I then asked who this lady was who was watching the two of you from the window. The answer I got was that she was your wife."

I didn't realize but my eyes had widened, and I was at the edge of my chair. "What happened then Helen? Who was the lady with me then?" I asked anxiously.

"The lady with you was another woman whom you thought you were in love with. Your wife in that lifetime, Rahul, was Maaya," she said looking at me straight in the eye.

I felt my heart sink while I heard this. I didn't want to hear more but I had to...that was the only way. "She knew you were cheating on her, but she didn't confront you. She feared losing you by exposing you. She had heard that every day when she was out working for the family, you called this other woman to be with you. She never dared to face this truth, for that needed her to have the courage to witness her own heart breaking. I think she was in some sort of denial. That day she incidentally came back home to fetch something when just before she could open the door, she heard the giggle of this other woman. She couldn't bear the sight, but she could no longer run away from the truth too. She decided to watch the two of you making love. It tore her into pieces, but it released her from her denial. She stood at the window with tears dropping from her eyes, watching her world getting shattered right in front of her. She was numb, blank and lost. Her eyes were open, her ears could hear and yet all she could feel was the hollow sound of infinite dark space."

I could almost feel exactly like Helen said, the hollowness of infinite dark space. As if there was only nothingness for as far as my thought could go. I didn't know what to say. I then knew that my vision was true.

"Do you want to hear it further Rahul?" Helen asked touching my hand. "Yes... hmmm," is all I could utter.

"Finally, when she could take it no more, she turned her back and sat down on the floor with her back against the wall, beneath the window. She cried profusely but pressed her cotton saree in her mouth to suppress her sobs from reaching your ears. She didn't want you to know that she knew. She tried to get up and leave but her legs were numb and weak. With each moan of yours, she seemed to die a little. Only after you had finished your act, you heard her cries."

I could almost feel a pain arising in my chest when I heard this. I didn't know what to do. "You became sober and quickly ran to the window to closely hear if what you had dreaded, had indeed happened. When you realized that the window was open and someone was sitting near the door, a chill ran down your spine. You opened the door and there she was. She looked at you with dead eyes. You were pushed into an ocean of shame where there was absolute stillness and no hope of breath.

This other woman saw her and quickly left the scene. You lifted Maaya from the floor, held her by her shoulders and took her inside to sit on the bed. She looked at the crumpled bedsheet and instead chose to sit on the floor next to the bed in silence. You left the house and closed the door behind you since there was nothing left to say," shared Helen.

"Helen, what happened after that?"

"Unfortunately, Rahul, I don't know any further. I was told that Maaya left her home and family forever that night. What happened to you or your family or her after that night, I cannot say. As for now, this is all that you must know. From that lifetime, you have deep rooted guilt of having chosen another woman over her when you in fact loved her. You also carry the guilt of putting her through so much grief and pain that she had no choice but to leave you and go," said Helen.

"Helen, this is exactly what I am feeling these days. I feel responsible for her leaving me because I gave her so much pain and grief that the only way for her to deal with it was to leave and go. I wonder many times in the current life too that if Maaya is all that I have ever wanted in a woman then why am I stuck with my wife and why am I doing all this? What is the purpose? Why do I get trapped in this situation over and over? There must be a way to break this pattern, Helen? If I had already lost her in that lifetime, shouldn't I have held on to her in this lifetime? Why do I keep losing her again and again?" I said, anxiously looking at Helen to say something to calm me down.

"Rahul let me heal this memory for you. Let me bring this recognition in your energies that whatever happened in that particular lifetime would have had some very good reason for it to have happened. This will bring more acceptance in you of your current situation." She then drew her chair closer to hold my hands again and we both closed our eyes. While she healed me, I felt tears dropping from my eyes, for I could feel what Maaya had been going through since maybe several lifetimes.

When she opened her eyes, Helen handed me some tissues. It was awkward. "It's okay Rahul. Vent it out. Let it all go. That's the purpose. If you carry this guilt of failing her, from this lifetime or beyond, you will stay entrapped in this pattern where all that you can give her is more failure. She doesn't need your failure. If there is anything, she needs from you, it is love. You will have to empty yourself of this guilt to be able to create a space for love in yourself. That's when she can enter your life and energies again."

"We are done for today Rahul. I want you to now observe your emotions, thoughts and experiences for the next two weeks. As we start aligning ourselves to a higher perspective, we start feeling differently about life. It then triggers a chain reaction where life also starts to present us with newer opportunities to experience the newfound alignment and to create more. All you must do is to witness yourself while being yourself, as much as you can. Let's now meet in two weeks," saying which she stood up and walked me to the door.

That was a long night. I was wondering how I had been so ignorant about this sub-conscious aspect of myself. On the other side I was wondering if I was hallucinating. What if none of this was true? What if she only told me some story that was emotional enough to convince me that it really was my past life? Hundreds of different thoughts cropped up in my mind. I wanted to believe but it wasn't easy. If I did believe, it made me feel ashamed and naive.

I was always sure that going to work, earning money, chasing desires and having someone to share yourself with was the complete definition of life. Maaya always tried to introduce me to my subtle side but I never accepted that there was anything other than my mind that could define my existence. I regretted never listening to her. I also wondered if it was her awareness of her deeper self that brought her loneliness and pain in life.

What Helen shared with me had left me with a question I decided to ask her the next time we met. I wanted to understand what my motivation had been each time to be drawn to another woman. If what Helen said was right, we create our own soul plans before we come to an earth life. I began wondering why I had chosen this situation yet again, where my marriage became another reason for Maaya and me to not be able to find togetherness in this life either. Why did I not create a plan where I could be with her?

Once I reached my apartment and changed, I took some time to introspect. The entire scene that Helen described was so vivid in my mind. I had been there. I had marred her soul.

As I thought about it, I scribbled these lines in the notepad lying on my bedside.

Maybe...

Maybe I was naive,
I didn't stop you when you left,
Maybe I was arrogant,
I didn't love you when you wanted,
Maybe I was selfish,
I wanted you to trust me even when I wasn't around for you,
Maybe I was unfortunate,
I let you go even though a part of me left with you,
Or maybe I was chosen,
Who else would be loved the way I was,
Yet would give it up for nothing!

Reading what I had written made me even more anxious. The solace that I had chosen had now transformed into the anxiety of having lost what I had. A gloom dawned on me.

That night ironically, I slept well. Helen had told me that since old memories are released through healing and the energies become lighter, one internally feels more relaxed and sleeps better. I woke up fresh as if with renewed energy. Before this, on most occasions when I thought about my personal life, either I felt hopeless and sad or I wanted to just look away from it. I mostly immersed myself in work. That day, there was some sort of acceptance which affirmed that my life wasn't exactly sorted, but at least I was headed in the right direction.

□

The Encounter

For the next few days, I felt calmer within. My curiosity about my past had increased though I felt more settled. I was able to focus on my work better, and I was looking forward to my next appointment with Helen.

I was to meet Gagan over lunch one afternoon. I was not expecting him to share Maaya's coordinates with me. I was nonetheless curious to meet him. He sent me the name and location of a restaurant. It was close to my workplace, so I walked up to it, managing to reach 10 mins before time. It was an upscale Chinese diner. I knew from Maaya's conversations that Gagan had fine taste, though this was the first time I was meeting him informally. She was most certainly right.

"Hello Rahul!" I heard from my side.

"Hey Man! What's up?" he said, as I stood up to shake hands with him, sounding like I was some old buddy of his. He didn't seem to approve of me the last time we met at his office. I wasn't sure what made him change his heart, but it was a welcome change. Seeing a smile on his face made me feel at ease in his presence.

"I am fine Gagan. Singapore is a warm place," I

responded. "Yup! I am glad you think so. I love Singapore which is why I keep coming back here. I am lucky that our firm attracts a lot of business from here which makes it easier and affordable," he said with an evident fondness for the city.

"I hope you didn't mind that I didn't ask you your preferred cuisine and just booked this place. I love this place, so I took the liberty of inviting you here."

"Oh no! Not at all. This place is stunning. I couldn't have made a better choice. Plus, I love Chinese food so it's cool," I said feeling pleased with the plush interiors and the subtle fragrance in the restaurant.

"Maaya also loved this place as much as you do," Gagan said very casually.

"Where is Maaya?" I popped the question crossing my fingers. The familiar sinking feeling in my heart suddenly reappeared.

"I don't know Rahul. It's not my prerogative to tell you unless she asked me to. I cannot choose for Maaya. She will meet you when she chooses to. For now, you must walk your path alone. If you are worthy, you will be guided in the most amazing ways and will meet her when it's time. I am only a witness to this divine play. I can only help you by walking along and offering my support. To find the right direction will be up to you," saying which he raised a toast.

I hardly knew Gagan. He was revealing a new facet of himself which I was unaware of. He seemed to be a nice guy though I always judged him. I had disapproved of him unnecessarily.

"Gagan, can you at least tell me if she is in Singapore?

Or if she has moved on?" I still asked him out of desperation.

"Rahul trust your gut. You will know if she would have moved on or not. Even if she has, you can hardly blame her. Don't attempt to possess her anymore. I would suggest you instead attempt to understand her, accept her wishes and recognize her role in your life. The need to possess someone often puts us in a never-ending chase. In the end, one might end up with what they chased, but since they never understood why they wanted it, they mostly fail to appreciate what they get. I think you need to find her place within you first. When you will pay attention, you may learn that there is none. You will need to empty some space by letting go of what is redundant. Once you can do that, you will attract her in the highest way. That's how the universe works through us. You just need to trust and allow."

There was so much similarity between what Gagan said and what Helen said. I knew that my relationship with Neha was still complicated. Moving on and away from her and bringing clarity within myself was imperative to invite Maaya back into my life. It was clear to me that Neha was not the one for me, and life with her lately had become a misery for both of us. It was Anushkha who had kept me hooked to my marriage. No matter how hard I tried, I was unable to see myself as the father who could abandon his child for his own selfish reasons. I don't know why I brought this up with Gagan. Maybe I was seeking approval from him or expecting him to at least understand me.

"I know what you are saying, and I completely resonate with you. I am just too scared for my daughter. I cannot come to terms with letting her go. That is one aspect that

I have not been able to address in spite of trying very hard. Don't you think it'll be extremely selfish of me to choose Maaya or my happiness over my daughter's interests?" I asked Gagan.

"Rahul, what if your unhappiness is all she gets to live through you? What if she grows up to ask you why you stuck around if you were so pained? What if she decides when she's old enough that she didn't need to be pitied? What if she has chosen self-empowerment by dealing with life as a child who comes from separated but responsible parents? Why can't you love her without having to live with her? Why can't you see that you might bring more value and meaning to her life by standing up for your happiness than by choosing self-sabotage and its consequences on those who are impacted by unwanted choices?

Children often don't learn what they are taught. They learn what they witness while no one is trying to teach them. She will learn from what you make of your life and not what you want her to see it as. You don't want her to learn that life is about sadness, lack of love and misery, do you?" he said.

What Gagan said was true and it struck a chord with me. I realized that I had never thought about how my sadness was anyway impacting my daughter's life merely by her witnessing me. If she had picked up brushing her teeth twice a day just because I did so, there must have been other things she was learning through my behavior which I was oblivious to. I was indeed perceiving Anushkha to be weak. Of course, she needed me, like each child needs their parents but that doesn't convey their being less. It was possible that she was a soul who had chosen me with my conflicts, only to grow wiser and stronger. I could only contribute better to her life if I was less disappointed with myself. The judgement I carried for myself prevented me from constructively spending time with her.

"Thanks, buddy. This helps. I will bring more clarity within on this aspect. Perhaps you are right. I have been thinking about this only from a moralistic standpoint. My indecisiveness could be doing my daughter more harm than good." I said to Gagan.

He nodded in agreement.

"What do you do apart from your work, Gagan? Where did you gain all this wisdom from? I have lately realized that maybe I have lived life pretty much on the surface so far. There is a whole new and fascinating world out there which one can experience even without touching or feeling it. I went for a therapy session here in Singapore. It was amazing. I have been feeling more sensitive to my emotions and more aware of myself ever since. I feel different." I shared with him.

"That's awesome. I am glad you took this step. A journey within is exactly what you need. That's what will help you the most.

With regards to what I do other than work, I run a *gurukul* for young children in Coimbatore. I do *sadhana* that keeps me aligned to deal with worldly matters and yet stay in awareness of my higher consciousness," Gagan said, to my surprise.

"A Gurukul"? What's that? I mean how? Since when?" I was amazed.

"For a few years. Rahul, a lot of us get introduced to our depth through some sort of loss. I also went through something that made me realize that I am a spiritual being who's trying to have a human experience. From that point onwards, I live my human experience fully, however I stay rooted in my spirit. It helps me fulfil my role and responsibilities and still stay in awareness of the ever-changing reality within and around me.

I believe it was a role to run this *gurukul* where young children are taught the ways of the soul. They gain not only all the knowledge required to make it big in the material world, but the awareness of their spirit is also enhanced so that when faced with adversity, they can stay still grounded and fulfil their role. It's in Coimbatore where I found my guru and got introduced to my higher self," he said.

"Wow! I must admit I have always been so judgmental about you. Maaya always spoke very fondly of you and it is only now I can see why. However, I always felt that this was merely her perception, for she was naïve and very unassuming. I'm now sure she was right. I am glad we met today as I have much to learn from you.

When I was in my late teens, I used to be a very loving and helpful person. I stood up for my friends and cared for everyone around me. My friends, family and neighbors used to count on me. I used to enjoy being this person so much that it was not even the least bit of effort. Slowly, I started realizing that I didn't get the same sort of reciprocation in relationships. I felt used and abused by those I trusted. I started to protect myself by interacting less, staying distant from people and staying focused on my work. I didn't even come to know when I had become so weary of people and relationships that it started reflecting in my personality and behavior.

Then Maaya happened. She was able to penetrate my soul. She was able to touch the person who was hiding within me. She made me feel loved and vulnerable at the same time. On the one hand I felt free and alive but on the other hand, I felt fearful and exposed. She and I had to part ways when she got married to Kunal. We had chosen different paths. This separation made such a deep impact on me that I became completely closed. I couldn't henceforth connect with anyone at the same level. Even though I married, and I did love my wife, something about that relationship was always more about my duty of being a husband than my love or connection with her. I never allowed her to reach the depth in me which was concealed even from me.

As destiny would have it, Maaya reappeared and what timing! This happened just when I was beginning to accept that life is a series of compromises and there isn't any love that's needed to fuel it. I had decided that aspirations and material desires are good enough to motivate one to live a decent life.

She rekindled the hope of love in me. She rekindled the part in me that I had become oblivious to. What I felt for her or what I felt about myself while she was with me was what I could never feel otherwise. It was so beautiful."

"Then what went wrong?" enquired Gagan.

"I was scared. The more love I felt for her the more fearful I became of losing her, or being without her, of my destiny, of everything. The courage and conviction I saw in her with regard to us, life, togetherness, love and truth were missing in me. I started fearing her for revealing my weaknesses to me. I couldn't tell her that I didn't believe enough in myself to be able to create love or beauty within. I couldn't tell her how I felt I would destroy her innocence and purity, had she chosen to be with me. I couldn't tell her how incapable I was of choosing love. I couldn't tell her how the depth of emotion that I saw in her eyes for me could drown me.

I didn't realize then that my fears had started to consume me, as though I had all that I could have ever wished for and yet I was willing to give it up. Just when I was going through this conflict, Neha reappeared with my daughter Anushkha back into my life.

Perhaps I used these fears as an excuse to distance myself from Maaya, since I had in fact always felt small as compared to her. She was too strong, too honest and was so full of love that it made me long for her while also making me feel unworthy. I didn't realize how and when I sabotaged the most endearing experience of my life. I knew that the way Maaya loved me, no one ever could. I knew the way she could accept my flaws and my weaknesses, no one ever could. I just didn't know if I deserved her. I have become too distanced, too disconnected from the source of love within me. When I seek Maaya, I am seeking that connection. However, whenever I have been able to experience that connection, it scares me. I become this person whom I don't know. I fear being hurt and losing it all. I fear destroying her innocence. I fear being myself for I feel that will destroy the love between us.

The real me is a cowardly escapist, distrusting and unsure of my own self. Maybe that's why keeping her distant from myself was my only way to keep her close to me too.

I don't know if what I said made any sense to you. Honestly, I have not recounted my journey with this much clarity ever before. I think there is a lot about myself that I have realized while talking about it today," I said feeling embarrassed about my admission of my truth.

Before Gagan could respond, I said, "Its ok. Let me be. I don't know why I said all this; however, it has helped me. Thank you for listening to me," looking down at my feet.

"It's good that you said all this. It helped me understand your dilemma. Maybe I can help you since I now know where you are stuck. You are afraid of your own power," he said with a lot of surety and calmness.

"Afraid of my power? Ha ha...I wonder what makes you say that," I laughed.

"Yes! When one is running away from self, they are running away from the power that'll be revealed if they accept themselves. It's as simple as that. We seek power externally while shying away from the source of infinite power within. I have often wondered why human beings choose power over empowerment," Gagan said.

"That's an interesting thought! Maybe power is visible while empowerment isn't?" I argued. We discussed many such concepts that helped me get insights into some concepts I had never tried to redefine before.

It was difficult for me to feel totally at ease with Gagan because my non-acceptance for him was deeply rooted for unknown reasons, but in all honesty, I did feel quite comfortable with him for the first time in my life. I realized he wasn't exactly how I had perceived him all this while.

That week, I had another new experience, courtesy my office mate Wee. He invited to me to a meetup. He insisted I accompany him at least once, so I obliged.

We walked into the meetup hall of the Galileo Healing Centre at 6:00 p.m. one evening, where some spiritual seekers had fixed to come together. They had regular meetings there where each week a guest speaker was invited to share their insights with the group. The meetup was organized by my colleague, Wee Cheng.

The hall was big with an ethnic décor. The enigmatic fragrance of essential oils filled the room. The ambience made me feel relaxed and comfortable. There were chairs laid out around the round tables that could seat about 5 people each. There were a few people who had arrived before me while we were waiting for others to come. I joined the table where only one guy was sitting. As I sat, he looked at me with a smile.

"I am Dan," he introduced himself.

"Hello. I am Rahul," I said while I made myself comfortable on the chair next to him.

"You have come for the first time, is it? What brings you here? Never seen you in any of the meetups," he said. "Oh! I didn't know these happen regularly. I was invited by Wee, since we work in the same organization. Just learning about this stuff, so I thought it might help."

Dan was a tall, well-built man with broad shoulders and a lean, muscular built. His eyes gave away his oriental roots, but his body shape and tight angular jawline conveyed European genes too. His face was fair, stiff as if molded from granite. His brows were light brown, sloping downwards in a serious expression, revealing the hard line around his lips more prominently.

"Yes, you never know what might help," said Dan with a smile, turning around just as the guest of the day arrived. She was an elderly lady who had been into mediumship and occult for twenty five years and she was going to share her experience of working with spirits.

From her demeanor, one couldn't miss her polite calmness, the one that builds over time as one slowly imbibes difficult life lessons to exude an evident wisdom.

It was an interesting session. Though the topic wasn't of much interest to me, I was slowly being initiated into a new world. She talked about her journey and one statement of hers struck a chord with me. She shared that it was the biggest lesson that she had learnt through her own journey that "My love for another person, however devoted or sincere it might be, cannot transform him or heal him of his inherent fears. The more I try to change him for his sake, the more enervated I become. My liberation is in freeing myself of my fear of his failure. My fears for him are about me. My worry for him is about me. His transformation that I want to see in him is also about me. My love for him is the source of my transformation through him and only that is my responsibility. The change his being will experience can be inspired by my transformation but it will never be a response to my expectations."

Dan and I had exchanged numbers and decided to meet up some day for lunch since we found out that we worked in the same building.

Often such experiences pushed me into a corner. I started to question if I was really carved for spirituality. I had a mind which was grounded in science and logic. I couldn't deny that I was having extra-ordinary experiences and the most bizarre coincidences, yet, something in me kept resisting anything that was not based on science. It was a constant struggle for me to try and understand if I was becoming one of those people who saw and felt energies and trusted the invisible more than the visible; or was I doing it all only to proclaim that I had been there, had done it all, and was hence gratifying my ego. I was not sure whether I trusted these processes or was hoping to experience some sort of magic.

Quite frankly, I didn't even believe in magic. During the sessions when I meditated for the first time, it was just so tough! I was asked to simply observe my breath and that's when I realized how challenging a simple task like that could be. Not just my breath, I could also witness so many thoughts. I couldn't manage to keep my eyes closed for more than five minutes. It in fact, landed me with a severe headache that lasted for the entire evening and I decided that it wasn't my cup of tea after all. My inability to meditate made me resist these sessions, some of which I had actually begun to enjoy. A few subjects which I was keen on exploring were ancient scriptures, mythology and history. Dan helped me then by convincing me to practice watching my breath for only five minutes by the stopwatch for twenty-one days. He reckoned that not only would I start enjoying it, but also be able to effortlessly increase the time of my meditation. Initially the headache reappeared, which was discouraging but as I persevered for a few days, the process became smoother. Dan was right, and I slowly started enjoying it to the extent that my thoughts didn't trouble me as much. I wasn't having any deep experiences, but just watching my breath with my eyes closed for a few minutes seemed to reset my system, clearing away all the cluttered thinking I had indulged in. I started to practice meditation more because in those moments, my mind felt strangely blank or thought free.

I was getting familiarized with spiritual practices. I witnessed people relying on various holistic approaches to deal with their lives. I couldn't completely fathom the idea of living in surrender to anyone or anything and yet, though I tried to understand and believe. My mind didn't allow me to be completely bowled over, yet I was addressing my resistance.

□

The Bali Escapade

I was squatting near a plant, watching it intently. I had no recollection of how it magically appeared at the opening of my cave in the highlands. It was strange since I was sure it wasn't there the previous day and it suddenly showed up, being at least 10 inches tall. Maybe these were the ways of these mystical lands, I thought. My recent experiences had taught me how to accept the unacceptable.

There was a certain calmness I felt as I touched its leaves. It almost made me feel as if I was touching life that is subtle and yet so evident. I had an eerie feeling, as if I could talk to this plant and it could hear me. I had not spoken to a single soul in over several days, so it wasn't a bad proposition.

The loneliness was grave and the constant fear that whatever I was running away from was waiting to haunt me all over again, was even worse. The silence outside created a very intense recognition of the void inside and sometimes I was able to tell myself, "It's ok to be alone." However, at most times the pain and hollowness that came with the void was such that I wondered if I'd ever be able to smile and laugh the way I used to.

I was becoming more and more sensitive to everything. I could hear noises I had never paid attention to. I could feel the flowers, the trees, the soil, the water and the sun rays differently. I had started to feel some unreasonable sort of joy within, and along with it, a grave sadness which also seemed to have no real reason.

Just then the air hostess nudged me, asking "Sir, would you like something to drink?" showing me the menu card. That's when I realized, I had been dreaming about my Bali escapade while resting on my lounge chair on my return flight from Bali to Singapore.

I ordered for a red wine and sipping it, reminisced the trip I was returning from.

It was some sort of gut that made me make the decision of spending 21 days at a campsite in the middle of the forest somewhere in north Bali. This expedition was a part of a meditation retreat in which we were made to spread out on the highlands dotted with old natural caves at different altitudes. We were trained to live alone and deal with life while spending our time meditating, introspecting, connecting with nature and witnessing our response to different kinds of situations we were bound to experience. The choice was between spending all twenty-one days by ourselves, not seeing or communicating with each other for the entire period of three weeks or meeting up every fourth day while spending the rest of our days in complete solitude. The five of us agreed upon the second option.

It was my first attempt at anything close to a planned endeavor to self-realization. The cave seemed big and cold. I had my camping material and all the stuff I needed to keep myself warm. The deal was that every morning before I woke up, the organizers of the retreat would keep the food for the day outside my camp. They wouldn't try to connect with me in any way because that would hamper my introspection process. In case there was an emergency, we were to fire air guns at the sky and the bright light they shot up would signal them to trace us from the site they were camped at nearby.

The highlands had wild animals and were surrounded by a dense jungle. We were given strict instructions to not venture out without a guide or a representative of the organizers. We could do that under supervision only on the day that all five of us were scheduled to meet, after every four days. Otherwise, we were meant to stay in or around our respective caves meditating, chanting or whatever it was that would help us deal with ourselves. The whole idea fascinated me so much that when it was offered by these organizers at one of our meetings through Wee, I agreed at once.

It had been a couple of months that I had been attending regular meetings and I had made some good friends. I had begun to enjoy this world where everyone was in acceptance of the fact that there is a higher intelligence that operates through all of us and that there are ways by which this consciousness can be harnessed to peace and joy within. I wasn't exactly sure if I felt it, however, being around all such people who were believers helped me stay in the belief that I was turning a tiny bit spiritual.

My regular sessions with Helen were also helping me in becoming more open.

When the mountain cave retreat was offered, only five of us agreed to do it- Leela, Dan, Gita, Heather and me. By then we knew each other by name and were acquainted with each other but sharing a trip together was a very different experience. We were all excited. I had met Dan once over lunch too but didn't really know him that well. I had been planning to take a break from work since I felt I needed more clarity about what I wanted in life. Only professional success and chasing clients or money wasn't giving me gratification anymore. I was now increasingly becoming aware that the seeking within was of something much bigger, but I was yet to understand what it was about.

The thoughts of Maaya had slowly taken a back seat. It's not that I didn't love her or crave for her. I sure did, however I had come to terms with the fact that I was not ready for her just yet, probably which was why she and I had not met again. There was some sort of knowing in me that the day I was sure of what I wanted and freed myself of the clutches of my inhibitions, Maaya would find me. It seemed as if she was watching over me and yet she wanted me to discover myself using my own free will. I didn't even know if this inner realization had any truth to it, yet it gave me solace and allowed me to stay focused on myself.

I had taken a month's leave from work and for the retreat experience to begin, we were to fly to Bali, Indonesia on our own.

The day I landed in Bali, the weather was exceptionally pleasant. I had been to the island several years back, but it had changed significantly. The old rustic feel was giving way to rapid modernization. The energy of the place was still as amazing though. I always felt more grounded and settled when I was on that island.

At the organizer's office, Leela, Gita and Dan were already waiting. Heather was yet to arrive. I greeted all of them and sat there waiting for further instructions. Heather arrived ten minutes later. Once our group of five was complete, Eric, the representative from the retreat organizer's office came to address us. We were handed over some camping equipment, some basic supplies of nourishing snacks, water bottles which could be refilled, gear to protect us against the weather, a gun to shoot in the air to raise an alarm, a torch and lots of small utility items. We had also been advised to bring some stuff that would help us sustain ourselves in the cave life for so many days. The good thing about the quest was that we were not expected to cook our own food. It was decided that when we met each other every fourth day, we could also not just interact with the organizers, but also collectively cook and engage in discussions, campfires etc.

Eric drove us in a jeep to a place which looked like a green forest with dense vegetation and a stream nearby. He asked us to find a good spot to camp anywhere within the next two miles. We were expected to walk on foot and explore the region to choose our spot that we would be spending the next three weeks in. Eric and his partner Yami had then earmarked all our locations to decide upon a central location for themselves so that they could reach us in case of an emergency.

They reckoned that though the area was the beginning of a forest, it was relatively safe. They also trained us on how to approach the situation if we happened to encounter an unexpected visitor from the jungle.

The purpose of this whole exercise was not only to reflect on our lives but also to overcome the fear of loneliness and recognize completion within self in so many ways.

We had not met Yami yet, but Eric told us that he would join us by the afternoon. It was still around 11 a.m. in the morning and we all were tired since we had flown in the same morning and the place was another two hours' drive from their office.

I finalized on a spot which naturally looked like a cave. It was quiet, pleasant and the stream was only a couple of minutes away. It seemed like a very apt location and I was sure that I was going to enjoy camping there. I had used the compass on my phone to realize that sunrise would happen right ahead of the opening of the cave while sunset would happen right behind. There were tall trees around but the view for both the sunrise and sunset seemed to be clear. There was a big rock just outside the cave, and this was where I decided I could do my meditations.

Eric had a walkie-talkie using which, he communicated with Yami. We were not allowed to carry phones or any other gadgets. Before dropping us at our respective camp sites, Eric collected our phones and switched them off. For these 3 weeks we were meant to disconnect from the world and just be with ourselves. At around 500 meters, Leela's camp was the closest to mine. The others were spread out further. As per the rules we were not allowed to venture out to socialize with each other. As decided, only on the fourth day could we meet and communicate with each other. And the twentieth day would be when we would camp together, enjoying the night sharing our experiences and take-aways, before leaving the following day. All of us looked excited and nervous at the same time.

I didn't know either of them well but Leela seemed the friendliest to me. Dan appeared to be lost in some thought process of his. Heather and Geeta seemed to know each other. Both appeared to be warm and friendly. As I stepped out of the jeep to finally take all my stuff and get dropped at my site, Leela gave me a particularly intense and nervous look and said, "You take care Rahul!" I wasn't sure what to make of it, since I felt I saw something in her eyes that I didn't quite understand. I decided to make nothing of it and just nodded my head with a reassuring smile. I shook hands with Dan, greeted Gita and Heather and got off at my spot, handing over my phone to Eric. I was the first to get off at my chosen spot.

Eric helped me put up my tent, gave me some tips and then he jumped back on the jeep to drop the others. Though there was a natural cave where I was camping, I still wanted to erect my tent just at the opening of the cave, so that I could feel cozier and better covered from all sides at night. I was anxious, excited and exhausted all at once. The tent in the shade of the cave with cold breeze touching me, seemed to be inviting enough for me to lie down and take some rest. Eric had handed me three meal packets for the day, and I was anyway stocked with some snacks and 2 bottles of water. The bottles they had provided us with had an inbuilt purifier and ionizer fitted in. We could use the water from the flowing stream nearby for drinking as the bottle would make sure that the water was hygienic enough to drink. Using that mechanism, I could refill my bottles until my next trip to the stream. The only thing I had to take care of was to use fresh clothes judiciously or wash them every other day. I wanted to make sure washing them was required minimally. I had enough tee shirts to last me the entire duration if I was careful.

When I woke up after a nap, the sun was already setting. I didn't realize that I had slept that long. However, I felt refreshed after waking up. The weather was beautiful, and I decided to light a fire. Eric had told us that the best way to keep animals at bay was to sleep at night with a fire lit outside. It would help keeping warm and in case needed, we could heat some food.

I walked up a few meters from my camp towards the rock and beyond to realize that I could see the city at a faraway distance with a sea of lights lit throughout. It was a stunning view. The whole experience so far had been enthralling.

Slowly the chill began to increase, compelling me to wear my old duffle coat, friendly and soft. I was hungry and had not eaten anything other than the sandwich which was served to me on the flight earlier that morning. I searched for the bag of food that Eric had handed me to see what I had to eat. To my relief the food still smelled good. There were three nicely packed meals. In one, there was a bacon and cheese sandwich. In the other, was rice and chicken curry while the third had strawberry flavored yogurt and some salad. It was perfectly packed since it remained fresh for all those hours. Besides, the cold and windy weather helped.

Famished with hunger, I decided to eat the salad as well as the bacon sandwich. That would have left me with the chicken curry and yogurt for my late evening meal since I knew I wouldn't be able to sleep again soon. The food would come handy.

I was happy with the meal and thought that if I only had my iPod to listen to some good old Hindi songs, it would have been the perfect evening. However, I knew that enjoying myself was the intent but not through external means. I had to stay focused on inner exploration, though that was the challenging bit. The silent surroundings and the fact that I was to spend three weeks all by myself there, made me intensely anxious within. Time was moving excruciatingly slowly. Everything was so alive, yet so silent. I had brought it upon myself to face this time alone but was doubtful that I could make it.

Brushing away my thoughts, I sat on the rock to meditate. It was peaceful and calm. Slowly the sun had set, and there was complete darkness. I could hear crickets and various other sounds. I didn't mind the noise so much, as it kept me company. Absolute silence would have been more difficult to deal with. I decided to hear the sounds with my eyes closed and just allow myself to witness my surroundings without really looking at them. Slowly the sounds started to fade away and the deep silence within led me to absolute darkness, as if I was inside a black hole. I felt I was going deeper and deeper into some sort of abyss.

I was so lonely in the huge dark world inside me,

feeling lost and directionless. I felt a need for someone to hold me, to say to me, "I am there."

"I am there Rahul," I felt Maaya whisper in my thoughts. Tears started to roll down. No matter how brave I became, I missed her immensely. I pined for her to be there, with me, sharing her wisdom with me. She was needed now more than ever. Nothing could have made me leave everything and travel all the way to a forest in Bali in self-search had it not been for my resolve to become worthy of Maaya.

Several thoughts in me questioned if it was all worth it. What if she didn't care? What if I was suffering for nothing? What if she had already forgotten me and created a new life for herself? In those moments I felt angry at her. I was angry that she had vanished, and in some way, it justified that I shouldn't feel so much at fault. I would justify myself, thinking that at least I told her the truth and I didn't say anything I didn't mean; I told her when I couldn't do what she expected me to do. I also proved myself right by thinking I was fair in trying to work my marriage out, because after all, even she felt that if there was a chance that my marriage could be saved, for the sake of Anushkha it should be my first choice. My mind eventually went back to thinking that if Maaya would have left her fiancé before her marriage and come to me, maybe our lives wouldn't have been so complicated. I also knew that I didn't really encourage her to do so at the time because my own mother wasn't too keen on me pursuing Maaya, which was something I never told her. So many conflicting thoughts, so much argument, blame, guilt and pain all together made me feel so vulnerable and helpless that my head started aching.

I felt I was getting sucked into my own darkness and it was consuming me. My own mind was my enemy. It didn't let me spend a few minutes in peace without these numerous debilitating thoughts.

I couldn't recall when I fell asleep. The rays of the morning sun hit me, making it uncomfortably warm to sleep anymore. I recalled feeling dizzy during the meditation but couldn't remember anything after that. I woke up in a haste, realizing that I had slept near a forest, with no precaution of any sort. The thought itself was scary. Yet, I felt better to have awakened to witness a beautiful sunrise. It was most likely the first sunrise that I was being conscious and aware of.

I had seen sunrises before, only because the window of my room opened towards the east; the moment the sun would start rising each morning, my first response would be to pull the curtain only to go back to sleep. I had never ever spent a minute extra standing there, witnessing and appreciating its beauty. That day, however, it was different. I felt soaked in the golden rays of the sunlight and every cell in my being felt alive with the recognition of a new day, a new morning and a new beginning.

I had to freshen up. We had already been given instructions on how to dig a hole, poop and then cover the hole. Thankfully I had carried enough toilet roll along and my choice of habitation had ensured enough water for hygiene by way of the stream nearby. I did my chores and was soon ready for breakfast. Just then I wondered if I my meals had been delivered.

I quickly checked up on the chicken curry I had left

over last night. I wasn't quite sure if it was alright to eat it since meat doesn't stay fresh that long. Just then I saw that there was a packet lying just next to my tent opening which didn't seem like I had seen it before. I quickly picked it up and opened it. It had my three fresh meals for the day. This was amazing. I didn't know how Eric and Yami managed to do this. Did they prepare fresh meals and deliver them early in the morning before sunrise? I guessed this couldn't be the case because the packet hadn't been there when I woke up. That's when it struck me that they put it there when I was away to freshen up. I was impressed.

The food smelled enticing and I now had a sandwich, a box with fish curry rice and a box of yogurt and salad with me. An additional snack of potato wedges was also packed saying "Just in case you cannot sleep." I decided to let go of the food from the previous day and keep it somewhere far from my camp for some animal to feed on it. I had fresh food in generous portions, good enough to get me through the day.

Once I ate, there was nothing more to do. This was when I started to realize how tough this escapade could be. I was yet to spend twenty more days doing nothing. I was not wired to do nothing. I had spent 35 years of my life constantly restless and always doing something. It was going to be challenging. It was ironical how not making any effort seemed more difficult than effort itself. This was my first observation. I took out the notebook I had carried to make notes about insights I could refer to later. It was my chosen way to acknowledge the changes that were happening within me.

I decided to walk up to the stream of water and fill both my bottles since I had almost emptied them. This would also be an opportunity to explore my surroundings a bit more and connect with it. The walk towards the stream was through some thick bushes. I just followed the sound of the stream and within 5-7 minutes I was standing there. It was a serene sight; I had never ever paid attention to natural beauty in my life. I was so consumed by my chase to be the best that I had never noticed how beautiful the world already was, and how ignorant I was of the evident serenity around me. I mentally made a note of this second observation. I was indeed learning, or maybe I was trying too hard? I didn't know but this conversation with myself was interesting. As I filled both my bottles with the clean water from the filter bottle, I saw a deer drinking water right opposite me on the other side of the stream. This stream was only perhaps 8-10 feet wide, but the flow downwards was steady. The deer was comfortable with me being on the other side, so it just continued to gulp water. It was so mesmerizing that I decided to sit there and just witness the flow, the life, the movement around me. I had started to enjoy this intimate experience with nature.

I wondered how different my life and experience would have been had Maaya accompanied me on this trip. I knew where my mind was going and I didn't want to sulk just yet, so I distracted myself by inspecting the area a bit.

As soon as the sun started to get a bit brighter, I walked back to my camp. I meditated for a while sitting on another rock on the back side of my tent, inside the cave. It was nice and cool inside the cave, so I enjoyed the moment of introspection before having my lunch. Post lunch, I took a short nap only to find myself sleeping till around sunset. I couldn't understand why I was sleeping so much ever since I had come to the forest. Helen would have said that I wanted to sleep over my free time and escape the self I had worked so hard to face. It was unusual for me to sleep so much. Just then it occurred that I had not even done my daily kriya and yoga all day long. I pulled out my yoga mat from my bag, spread it on the grass and stood over it, facing the sunset. This was the first time ever that I was doing yoga facing the setting sun. It was a breath-taking sight. I kept doing my asanas and in another 20 mins I sat down with my eyes closed to do my kriya. By the time I finished my kriya, it was twilight.

Having finished my daily meditation and yoga processes, I felt better about myself. I had never understood the logic behind it but doing these yogic practices at least once in a day kept me feeling energized and rejuvenated. They uplifted me with a fresh breath of life. Ever since I had learnt the Shambhavi Mahamudra, it had helped me tremendously in just staying more aligned and centered within. I had learnt this in India when a teacher from Isha Yoga center had conducted the Inner Engineering Program by Sadhguru in our company sponsored retreat. I felt good after doing the kriya and they insisted that one must follow the practice for at least 40 days. I complied and ever since, it had become a part of my routine that never left me. It had been over a year that I had been practicing it daily. I wasn't sure of its spiritual benefits, but it certainly made me feel more aware of my body. I was left feeling grounded, rejuvenated and stable. It was a big deal for me to be this way, especially with Maaya not being around.

Maaya...My thoughts suddenly drifted towards her. Once Maaya's thoughts started clouding my mind, I couldn't push them away. I often wondered where she would be and if she would be missing me as much as I missed her. I quickly tried to distract myself since I knew I was entering a dangerous territory. I didn't want to think about her because that could potentially lead me to recognizing that it was possible, she had forgotten me and moved on with someone else. Whenever these thoughts came, they left me feeling like a failure and I couldn't help but feel powerless. I reminded myself that I had come here to reclaim my inner power and resolve my life and not to get trapped in my fears. I had been reading a book just before I came to Bali, where the author had described how our fears were traps we created in our minds only to limit our power. She reckoned that any choice ever, is between faith and fear. While choosing fear comes more naturally and effortlessly, faith is what one must choose for growth. I had decided to follow her advice and each time I had a choice; I chose faith over fear. This approach was really helping me deal with a lot of my fears.

It was pitch dark again and I was yet to have my third meal. I realized that I couldn't find my meal without my torch since I could hardly see anything. It dawned on me that I was in a jungle or at least near one and it might be a good idea to light a fire. I somehow managed to locate the torch in my bag, lit the fire and located my food pack.

Having eaten food, I spent some time simply listening

to the insects around, just like the day before. Honestly, that intense experience into nothingness had left me intrigued and I wanted to continue that journey. However, I also didn't want to go to sleep on the rock in unawareness since I did realize that it was dangerous. Hence, I decided this time that I'd rather watch the moon while sitting on the rock but do the meditation inside my tent. Even if I went into deep sleep, I would be safely tucked inside my tent and the fire would keep any animals at bay.

I wrapped up everything, sat inside my tent and closed my eyes. Just before closing my eyes I closed the zip of my tent and allowed myself to focus on the sounds of the various insects and winds around me, slowly witnessing my breath.

This is when I noticed that I had been thinking of Maaya even more than ever since I came to the retreat, perhaps because this camp was the type that she would have loved being a part of, or maybe it was just that I was too lonely. At office, I had too much work and too many distractions, making it easier to avoid her thoughts, but I was alone here with all the time in the world. Her thoughts haunted me. My longing for love gaped at me every now and then. The thought of being alone at night, waking up to no one next to me, no one near me to speak with, to love, or to care for brought deep recognition of how important a partner is for one's sanity and wellbeing.

As I started to watch my breath, the chatter started to fade away and I started becoming aware of the dark nothingness within me. I became a silent follower of it, going deeper and deeper in. Suddenly, it felt as if I was reaching somewhere. As if that endless fall into the dark pit within me was eventually leading me to some place. My heart started beating faster and I started experiencing weird movements inside and around my stomach. I saw something at a distance in that pitch darkness. It made me anxious.

Suddenly, there was movement around my tent. I got pulled out of the dark pit back into my senses in a fraction of a second with a sudden jerk. I was blank, numb, shocked and afraid. I could hear movements as if there were some footsteps. Soon I saw a sort of shadow on my tent as if someone was standing close. I was so scared. While I was being cautious at one end to observe any further movement, my other hand was automatically already looking for the gun to fire in case of an emergency.

"Rahul are you there?" said a woman's voice from outside the tent. I dropped my defenses and opened the zip of the tent. "Leela! It's you. You scared the hell out of me. We weren't supposed to meet each other for another two days. Don't you remember?" I said to her while I stepped out of the tent to talk to her.

She said nothing but just hugged me tight and, in a few seconds, I realized she was sobbing. "Leela! What happened?" I asked, holding her by her shoulder and separating her from my chest. It felt odd since I hardly knew her.

"I feel so lonely and scared Rahul. It's like all my demons are haunting me. I am not sure I can deal with this. I feel everything and everyone that I am running away from is here. I can't sleep. I can't eat. I don't know how to calm myself down. I don't know how to meditate. My thoughts are so overwhelming. Help me Rahul! Please help me!" she said sobbing even more.

"Okay Leela, relax! Have some water," saying which I offered her a place in my tent and made her drink some water. She looked pale and exhausted, as if from a lot of crying. "Leela, do you want to tell me your story? Maybe then I can help you," I told her. I realized that she needed to breathe and take it easy.

Keeping the glass down, she said "Yes, I want to Rahul. I think it will help me shed some burden off too. I really need to talk to someone right now."

I nodded.

"I come from a very conventional Greek family. I have many Indian friends, so I know that our value system is very similar to that of yours. I met a guy called Simon in the green city of Athens four years ago. We were both 22 years of age back then and we instantly fell in love. We got married within a year of dating. He was very nice to me and we both were perfect for each other. Slowly his love started to fade away. He started working long hours and avoided me sometimes. We stopped having sex that often. He was mostly irritated or tired, he wouldn't take me out anywhere and after a point he also started to become rude. I couldn't understand what was happening. I was a doting wife and I took care of all his needs and waited for him all day long only to eventually be shouted at for the pettiest of things.

Our families didn't live with us. I felt lost and confused. I didn't know how to interpret what was happening to us. I used to cry for long hours since I had no one to share my grief with. I didn't want to involve my parents since I knew they would get very anxious. I didn't want them to worry for me. Each time I tried to bring it up with Simon as to why he was behaving this way, he'd rather put all the blame on me saying he was normal, but it was me who bugged him because I had nothing better to do.

I felt my life had come crashing down on me. I had left my work in Patras to join him in Athens. He thought I was seeking attention from him since I had too much time to kill. I hadn't taken up a job as I wanted to be a housewife and make a family, but his taunts started to make me think of going back to work. Many times, I felt the problem was something else, as if it was deeper, but he avoided talking about it and the distance between us grew.

I loved him so much that the thought of losing him gave me a heartache. I didn't know what to do to set things right. My biggest problem was that I didn't know what exactly had led to this change in him. He was the most compassionate and caring guy," Leela shared.

"Did you eventually find out what was wrong?" I was curious.

"Yes, several months passed. I got used to being ignored, being treated rudely, yet I blamed it all on his work stress. One day he decided to speak up. He made me sit beside him and said his problem wasn't me. The problem was with him only. He didn't feel love for me anymore. He said that though he initially did have very strong feelings for me and he also found me attractive which was why he married me, things had changed since then. He didn't feel those emotions anymore and something inside him couldn't connect with me any longer. He said he had tried to fight that emotion within himself which is why he was constantly irritated and angry since he knew he was being unfair to me. However, he had realized that it was not working out and his disconnect towards me from within was so deep and so apparent now that he didn't want to keep both of us miserable. He had decided to let me go," she said with stone-like wide wet eyes looking at me.

Deep in my heart I recalled saying something on those lines to Maaya, when she had called me from Singapore. It hurt. She must have been devastated. My guilt started to consume me.

There was absolute silence for a minute or so. Then she took a deep sigh and continued.

"At first I couldn't believe what I was hearing. I couldn't believe this was the same guy who once cried so much in the middle of the night, hugging me and begging me to promise him that I would never ever leave. I was so taken aback that I couldn't say a word. I felt that saying anything was totally useless since it seemed he had fought the battle and lost it too, all by himself. I could perhaps beg him to not leave me, but I couldn't beg him to love me. If I still chose to stay with him, I would choose pain and unhappiness as my constant companion too.

I slept on my wooden rocking chair that night while still in disbelief and shock. When I woke up in the morning, Simon was gone. He didn't tell me where he was going. He just left a note saying, "Goodbye. Have a good life. I will send the papers," and that was it!"

It sure must have been extremely tough for Leela. She

had completely relied on this man for her life.

"Is this what brings you here Leela? Are you still stuck with Simon? Have you not been able to move on from him?" I asked.

"I am not sure Rahul, if it is Simon that I am stuck with. I think I am stuck with "rejection" instead. I am badly stuck with rejection. It sucks, it hurts, and it destroys!

I somehow attract it over and over. Ever since Simon and I got divorced, I have had four relationships but in each I have given more and received less, yet eventually I was the one who was rejected. It's like love is some obscure experience that I am chasing so desperately and yet each time that I feel I have reached it, it slips away even further."

I didn't know what to say. Leela sounded very upset and all I could do was to let her to cry. "Leela, I think you are a beautiful and kind-hearted girl. Sometimes we give a lot because we don't value ourselves so much. In my culture, I have seen several women getting hurt or abused only because they don't think they are worthy of love and acceptance. They continue to suffer in their existing relationships but refuse to stand-up for themselves and believe that they deserve better. You must recognize your worth. You must realize that these men who couldn't appreciate you despite you loving them enough, don't deserve you. You are waiting for someone better," I said.

What I said, somehow made her cry even more.

"I am not sure Rahul. I sometimes feel this is it, I don't have the energy or motivation to go on. I still think of him many times. My thoughts still drift away to those beautiful moments we spent together, holding hands, promising we would live and die together. It's as if time has not passed. I fear seeing him with someone. I fear I might have to live alone for the rest of my life. I fear no one can ever make me feel the way he did. I fear I am slipping into depression and I won't be able to pull myself out of my yearning for him," saying which she sobbed even more.

Leela was too exhausted so she just lay down silently while wiping her tears with the tissue I gave her and closed her eyes. I just let her rest in my tent while I chose to meditate on the rock outside my tent.

I knew when I walked out on Maaya, after having made all those promises to her, she also would have been devastated like Leela. I then recalled the several times when Maaya called me from Singapore or after coming back and while I was trying to be honest to her about my lack of feelings at the time, each time she ended up crying while keeping the phone down. My shame for devastating Maaya started to drain me and an abysmal sadness started gripping me again.

In some way, it felt slightly more comfortable that I was not all by myself. Leela's presence made me feel more at ease with my surroundings. My fear of going off to sleep while meditating on the rock was not there anymore. I sat on the rock, closed my eyes and focused on my breath for a few seconds. It again felt as if there was a swirl inside me, through which I travelled deeper and deeper down. It was dark and empty, just like swirling against the walls of a murky, dark well.

This time however, I managed to reach some sort of place. It was dark, dense and a little cold. Suddenly I saw the silhouette of a girl who seemed to be sitting on the ground with her head tucked between her folded knees. She was sobbing. I felt deeply saddened though I didn't know who she was. I went close to her and bent down to touch her on her shoulder. She raised her head and looked at me with big, beautiful but teary eyes. "Who are you and why are you crying?" I asked her. "You don't know me?" she asked with a curious look on her face. I was surprised because it seemed like she expected me to know her. "No, I am afraid I don't know you," I said to her. "That is why I am crying. You ought to know me, understand me, love me, embrace me and accept me," she said while still sobbing.

I was unsure of what she meant by this. Just then she raised her head again out of her folded knees and stood up. I stood up too. She looked at me intently while wiping her tears. "I am the feminine inside you. I am your feminine energy. I am half of who you are. I am who makes you creative, thoughtful and keeps you in touch with your inner world. You ideate through me, you love through me, and you touch your inner world through me. I am who helps you feel yourself," she said. I didn't understand any of what she said but somehow there was a deep sinking feeling in me, and I felt as if the whole ground on which we were standing started to shake. Suddenly everything started collapsing and she started to fall further into darkness, and I started to be pulled outward. I could hear her wail and cry, as if she wanted me to help but I had no control over this experience. Suddenly with a jerk my eyes opened, and I found myself sitting on the rock. My breath was extremely heavy, and I struggled for a few seconds to breathe properly.

My head felt dizzy and it took me a while to register my surroundings and come back to my senses.

I didn't know what this experience was and why the girl said what she did. I could still see visions of her crying and as if this was making me grieve, still I didn't know what to make of it. The whole episode had left me feeling incomplete and restless. I wanted to go back to her to understand what she meant when she said she is half of who I am. What was it that I did to make her so miserable? Neither was I able to forget the incident nor was I able to understand it. I didn't understand what her "being my feminine" meant?

Feeling drained and extremely exhausted, I decided to sleep over it. If I ate anything, there was a good chance I would have thrown up, so I decided against it. I drank a few sips of water, lit the fire outside, tucked myself in my sheets, zipped my tent and dozed off into a deep sleep on the opposite side to where Leela was sleeping.

I woke up post sunrise. When I checked my watch, it was about 9 a.m. already. I had slept for almost twelve hours, but I guess I needed to. I felt fresh. Leela had left, and I was hoping that she also felt better after a good night's sleep. The thought of the previous day's incident was lingering at the back of my mind, however, I felt much less restless than immediately after the experience.

Waking up to find no one around was a difficult reality to deal with. I was not sure if I was progressing to self-recognition or I was simply becoming a victim of my grief and sadness. I was having mood swings. One moment, I felt better while in another, I would feel miserable. I was not sure.

It was the fourth day, so we all were meant to meet at noon at a pre-decided spot in the middle of the highland. I was excited because I wanted to understand what the others were experiencing. Admittedly, I was also a little concerned for Leela. She seemed to be in bad shape. I hoped that she was coping better after last night. It was a relief that we chose to meet up at regular intervals. Staying alone all through the tenure could have been overwhelming for most. Every now and then the extreme loneliness had already made me question my choice of committing to the retreat. It was hard to not be tempted to just give up. I was looking forward to distracting myself from my mounting restlessness by meeting up with the others.

The place where we were meant to meet was about 700-800 meters from my tent. I walked up there to find that everyone had reached before me and they were waiting for me to arrive. Greeting everyone, I sat on one of the rocks. We were all sitting in a circle, some of us on rocks and some on chairs laid out there.

"We have been asked to start sharing our life stories with the group by Eric and Yami. They left a note here saying they will join us in sometime, while we can begin," Leela updated me.

There was silence. I guess the question was, who would go first. Just then Heather spoke.

"Let me bell the cat!" hearing which everyone smiled.

Heather was in her late forties, and she gave the impression of being a woman who lived life deeply. Her aura was intriguing, and her eyes glistened. She had volunteered to share her story, though I was not sure how open she or anyone would be about sharing their life story with a group of strangers. I noticed that she looked at all of us one by one as if bracing herself.

"I am not sure how or where to begin. I have always been curious about energies and how this universe functions. I often asked myself why I was here on this planet even when I was a kid. As I grew up, my interest in occult grew and I started to learn mediumship. I could communicate with spirits who have moved on and yet are stuck on this plane. I could understand people's emotions and thoughts without them saying a word to me. I could feel people and what was going on inside them when they were in my energy field. Initially all this was exciting but slowly it started to bother me. I started to feel entangled in my own intense sensitivity to other people's energies.

My relationships didn't last because I was hypersensitive, and I didn't leave any room for the other person to breathe. I assumed I knew what my partner wanted in the relationship and thus, the other's role was significantly minimized.

When I was twenty-four, I met Larry. He was also a sensitive guy and he was true to me. He did everything for me, better than what I'd expect from him. He took care of things for me without me even telling him to. He loved me and cared for me just the way I had always wanted. We lived in a small house with a large garden. He built a small saltbox shed for me in our garden where I could sit and do my healing practice or even call my clients when I needed to do a one-on-one session with them.

Larry mowed the lawn, removed the snow, took care of

the groceries, walked the dogs and did everything to make my life comfortable."

"Wow that sounds like the ideal relationship. You are lucky," Leela said to Heather.

"Yes, maybe I was! However, I was unhappy from within," she said to our astonishment.

"Really?" I said.

"Yes. You might find it weird but there was one aspect of my life that Larry could not help with. That bothered me too much," she said.

"What was that Heather? Was he not good in bed?" Leela asked inquisitively.

"No dear. He was like a dream in bed. We had the most erotic sex and he was able to satisfy me like no other," she said.

We all looked at each other and her. It didn't make sense. This guy seemed to be a dream not only for Heather but perhaps for any woman. What could that aspect be that left her feeling incomplete even with Larry? Everyone's attention was now on Heather. I noticed then that even Dan, who had seemed inattentive until then, now sat up interested in her story.

"He had no spiritual interests, whatsoever! From my childhood, I had grown up playing with energies and my life and conversations revolving around spirits, souls, mediumship, angels and astral worlds. I couldn't connect with him at that level. He was not interested. He was a gym guy and I was a yoga woman. He could listen to me for hours, but he couldn't participate in a conversation with me. I found it tough to connect with him through the means of a conversation. Having sex was easy for us but holding a meaningful dialogue where both of us would participate was difficult," she said.

"Hmmm," Leela let a confused acknowledgement escape her.

It seemed like Leela and I were the most enthusiastic of the lot. I wanted to know more. Just then Gita said, "What happened next Heather?"

I was glad that someone other than Leela and me was equally curious.

"I tried my best to engage him in my work, my interests, spirituality etc. but he was adamant that these things didn't interest him. He was happy for me to do whatever I was doing but he would rather stay away from it. This apathetic attitude towards the meaningful things in my life broke my heart every single day. I wanted the man I loved to be involved in my life, my thought process, and my way of perceiving things but alas that was not possible because Larry had put up a wall there.

Slowly this gap grew so big between us that we started to fight and argue. Eventually I realized that I would never be happy with a man who was so stuck on his viewpoint and it was not possible for me to give-up on what I had learnt because I had never known how to live life any other way. We parted ways after two years of being with each other and trying our best to work out our relationship. In every other way, our relationship was perfect, but the impediment was that we had chosen different paths for ourselves.

Although I was the one who walked out on him because

it was becoming suffocating for me, it took me three years to come out of the relationship. I healed myself every single day only so that the void that was there in my heart and soul for having found the perfect man and lost him, could be filled," Heather sighed.

All of us sighed though we had not realized this was not the end of her story. She continued without noticing that we had assumed she was done.

"Four years after breaking up with Larry, I came to know that he was in a relationship with another woman and he was practicing and teaching yoga with her," she said.

"Oh my god!" said Leela in bewilderment.

Heather looked at Leela with sadness in her eyes. "Yes, I was shocked and gravely hurt. No matter how hard I tried, I couldn't forget him completely. I couldn't forgive myself for being the way I was. I had failed since what he didn't choose to do for me, he did for another woman. As if my being brought me a huge loss, loss of love!

I had several relationships after Larry, but never could feel so complete again, until when I met Gaelic."

"Wow! So, you found true love again?" said Gita.

"Yes, I did. What people don't find even once in their lives, I found twice and both times it filled my soul with eternal bliss. Gaelic was the most compassionate man I had ever met. He was so gentle and yet so firm. He knew what he wanted, and he knew how to take care of his woman. He loved me and nurtured me like a rose. He knew all about my incompletions and my flaws. He knew the craving for love I carried deep within. He slowly and gently caressed my soul and filled my wounds. He was unbelievable in so many ways.

He was wiser than me and shared my interests. He had practiced shamanism and had been an apprentice of a Shaman in Eastern Europe for several years. He understood the body and its connection with subtle energies like none other. He taught me so much and perhaps also learnt from me. It was so complete to be with him," she said with her voice becoming heavy.

"So where is Gaelic now?" I asked her.

"Last year, one evening he finished construction work for the new greenhouse we had decided to build in our backyard. We were standing in the backyard and he was going to take a bath. He appreciatively looked at the greenhouse, the house and me and said, "I have done it all. Completed it. Haven't I?"

I gave him a kiss and said, "Yes you have darling! You have completed me in every way. Thank you."

"He went to bathe, and after that we made love. As soon as I felt the tender sweetness of his breath on my neck, while he had immersed himself in me, stiff and upright, he left his body. He died in my arms with a wide, beaming smile on his face," she said turning her face away from us only to hide the tears in her eyes.

There was complete silence. None of us could say a word. We were in shock and disbelief. I couldn't believe she was hiding so much pain behind that serene look of hers.

Heather wiped a tear and then looked at us saying, "I am not sad. What Gaelic gave me is beyond comprehension for most. He completed me. He did not leave a void in me. He left me with him in me. He is forever merged with me. Yes, I miss talking to him and touching him, but I don't experience his loss. He lives in me and grows through me each moment.

I am not here to overcome my loss because there was none. We both completed each other in every way. I am here because I now want to understand the purpose of my life further. I am unsure of what else lies ahead of me on this planet now. There must be a reason why I still live. I feel love and compassion for each being and I feel I can go on endlessly so what's the point? For the past few months, I have been seeking guidance for my journey further. I was guided to come here, as if to say I would understand my onward journey through this journey and here I am," she said with a smile.

Her spirit was amazing; her thoughts brought peace and closure to the unrest that surfaced when we all heard about Gaelic's departure. Gita and Leela gave her a hug.

Everyone then looked at Gita. Since she was sitting next, it was her turn to share what brought her to this retreat. After Heather's story, there was intense silence since everyone was in a sort of introspective mode.

"Hello everyone! I guess it's my turn now. My name is Gita and I am half Singaporean and half Indian. My mother is Indian while my father is Singaporean. I grew up in India and then Australia and very recently moved to Singapore.

I am not too proud of the way I have shaped up my life, but I will share it with all of you because I know that this is my only chance to release all that I carry, and I will need the help of each one of you to show me whatever I seem to be blind to. I have decided to let go of my veil for if I can't do it here, I may never be able to do it.

So, here you go!

My childhood was difficult because my parents constantly fought with each other about something or the other. I couldn't understand the purpose of them being married or staying together if it was so difficult. I was their only child and I had no one to turn to on those lonely nights when I was pushed into my room so that their fights didn't have a so-called bad impact on my mind. However, the impact was taking place, nevertheless. I was learning to fight because I was learning that only fighting would let me present my point since everything around our house ended up in a fight.

Somewhere I feel that my parents should have just parted ways when I was younger because that way the only impact it would have had on me would have been that I'd have to deal with being a child from a broken home. Nevertheless, if they still cared about me, which I felt they did, at least they would have had the opportunity to love me and for me to appreciate this. The way they lived together and suffocated each other, I couldn't appreciate their individual love for me because in my mind, they were separate, yet pretending to be together. They were imposing themselves on me as one unit while their tempestuous relationship with each other projected nothing of a unit, so the whole situation left me bewildered. I stopped believing in marriage and unison. I stopped believing in love between a couple and yet I think somewhere unconsciously I also started chasing it. I slowly became a rebel. I wanted to fight for everything, which meant I created situations which worked against me. I didn't understand any of this back then. At that time, I was engaged in believing that I was a victim of my parents and their failed marriage and this became my perfect excuse for my personality to only exude hostility.

My first relationship happened when I was in class eight in school. He was in my class and we both felt a spark when we accidently touched each other while exchanging a notebook in class. He pursued me, and we ended up going to his place after my tuition class while his parents were not at home, and we had sex. I am not sure if I enjoyed the experience but the rebel in me was happy, as if I had been able to avenge my parents by having my life in my control.

The next day when I reached school, all kids in my class were looking at me weirdly and a gang of boys looked at me and laughed. I didn't understand. My best friend then told me that this guy had shared our encounter the previous day with his friends and one of our teachers had overheard it. The guy I had slept with was called by the principal.

I still remember that I literally peed in my skirt upon hearing this. I didn't know what to do. I was also called to the principal's office and when I reached, my dad was already sitting there.

He didn't look at me and just kept staring blankly at the principal. At that time, we were living in Bangalore, India. It was a big deal for a parent to be told what my dad had been told. He didn't bring my mum along because she would have freaked out completely.

I was supposed to go back home with my father that day. It was perhaps the most shameful day of my life. I didn't know how to look at him in the eye. We were walking down the alley towards my home when suddenly my dad stopped me and looked at me. His eyes were full of tears and he said, "I have failed you my child. I have failed your mother too. I have failed myself. Please forgive me."

I didn't understand why he said what he said but I remember I was numb upon hearing it. I still do not understand my lack of emotion at that moment, but I simply stood there saying nothing.

The next morning when I woke up, my dad was gone. He left us and moved back to Singapore. I never understood why he did that, but I just remember that my mother was sitting stone eyed on the dining table and when I asked her what happened, she just said, "Your father has left us forever!"

I never saw my dad again. My mother became numb after my dad left us. Maybe she was too shocked at how he did it or too disappointed with herself for not doing so before him. She enrolled me in a boarding facility in North India and that's where I finished my schooling.

I was never good at studies, but I vented my lack of love from my parents through Karate. I slowly became pretty good at Karate and earned a lot of medals at inter-school competitions. Based on my sporting caliber, I got a scholarship to the University of Canberra, so I got a chance to move to Australia.

Slowly I started dating guys and during my four years in Australia, I had several relationships one after another. Each of these guys doted on me, but I was a commitment-phobic. I was alright partying with them and having sex but when it came to be getting serious, I would chicken out. I didn't want commitment, for I only saw it as a threat to my freedom.

I pursued Karate in Australia too but the faster I was running away from my emotions, the quicker I was losing my patience, my focus and my skill. I ended up fighting with people during practice or taking too much risk. When my coach tried to teach me better, I yelled at him too. I couldn't cope with the projection of strength while feeling weak and miserable inside. One day I just quit it. As if by giving up on Karate, I was punishing the world around me who was mean to me. As if it was their loss, not mine.

Eventually I started a job in sales and marketing at a big corporate firm and soon enough, I fell in love with my boss. He was ten years older to me. Well read, chivalrous, decent looking and an extremely charming man who was attentive to me. Initially I thought I had a crush on him, but when he also started paying too much attention to me, things started to become serious. He was married and had two kids. We started spending a lot of time together at work and then he started planning work trips where I would accompany him.

He said he loved his wife and would never divorce her. As per him, his relationship with me had an important role in his life but it eventually had no future. He made it very clear to me that he needed me more than he loved me. However, this was perhaps the first time in my life that I was chasing someone as opposed to someone chasing me. I was a rebel at heart so chasing gave me the thrill and this kept me longing for more to chase. I had trapped myself in a vicious cycle.

Slowly, I started feeling possessive about him. I started

feeling pained when I saw him talk to his wife and kids lovingly. I started to feel wronged when he booked a hotel room for us to go and have sex. I felt used, objectified and demeaned. However, he was just being who he was from the beginning. He had never promised to bring the stars for me or to be there for me forever. He was in an arrangement where two adults were spending time together and fulfilling each other's needs. He saw it just as that and was livid whenever I expected anything more out of our relationship.

I loved him, and he was the ideal man for me to want as my husband and father too. It was as if everything I wanted to see in my father, I saw in him. Now that I come to think of it, through him I was loving my father. Slowly it became more and more difficult for me to stay in the same office and be called his keep, behind my back. Also, I saw his complete disinterest in committing any more than a few hours every week to being with me. One day we had a big fight and I created a huge scene at work and just came back home.

I expected him to be mad, but I knew he would resolve this with me, since I had some fancy, misplaced notion in my head that though he was bound by responsibilities, he still did love me, even though he chose not to admit it.

The next morning, I was so happy when I called him to tell him that I was pregnant and before I said that, he told me "You are fired Gita. I don't want to see your face again. Get your desk cleared and your accounts settled before I come back from Jersey in a week. Goodbye."

I didn't tell him about my pregnancy. I somehow still believed he loved me, but it was me who pushed him to such limits that he had to let me go. This was the first time

I felt for someone so deeply ever since my dad left me. I wanted to hold on to the connection, thus I decided to give birth to my child.

I now have a 6-year-old daughter who studies in the same boarding school as I did, in North India. Just 3 months ago, I saw my ex-boss again, outside a hotel in Australia with his hands on the waist of a woman who wasn't his wife and just as with me, he had booked a suite to sleep with her in that very hotel. Seeing this shattered me completely. All these years I had loved my daughter and cherished my life as if I was loving what I had with him. Now suddenly I feel so much disgust for him and myself that I can't fathom how to deal with it. Ever since that day, I have been avoiding talking to my daughter on the phone and I feel as if I see a part of him in her and it hurts me. I also worry that I am pushing my daughter to grow up to become another version of myself who did everything only to get the acceptance and love her parents failed to give her, and ended up screwing her life.

Phew! That's it, guys. That's my story. Thank you for listening to me for I have never shared all this with anyone in one perfect flow, ever."

Heather got up from her seat and hugged Gita with utmost love and compassion. All of us were appreciative of the honesty with which she was able to express her life in such vivid details.

It also got me thinking about how we all have various challenges which make us feel trapped and unhappy. Everyone has something that is too much for them to deal with. It was all very heavy and yet so profound. I felt my love for humanity was steadily increasing and my heart was expanding.

Soon it was Dan's turn. He did realize that he was meant to speak however he was trying to avoid eye contact with anyone.

Dan was a quiet and reserved person with a stern look on his face. He didn't talk much.

"I am not too much of a storyteller. I am not much of a speaker either. I am not sure how ready I am to share my life right now, but all I have to say is that I am dealing with betrayal and hurt. The betrayal has pierced me deep and scarred my soul. I am unable to go beyond it. I am just trying hard to understand my lesson and what the right thing is for me to do next.

I don't feel like discussing it at this point, but I will when I am more ready. Let my wound heal a bit more for me to be able to talk about it," he said.

"Yes, it's perfectly alright buddy!" I told him.

Now it was my turn. I didn't honestly feel that I could do justice to my life and experiences by sharing them like this. Nevertheless, I felt it would help me get more perspective on it, so I started speaking.

"Ok, my turn! I am Rahul and I belong to India. I am currently on a work assignment in Singapore. I have never shared my life with anyone before, but I feel it will help me offload my burden by sharing it."

Leela, Gita and Heather nodded.

"I have loved Maaya, ever since eternity maybe, but in this life, from when I met her at a mutual friend's wedding while we were in our early twenties. She was the definition of love, care and compassion for me. She gave me so much love that in my pride, I forgot that she was the source of it.

When we met, she was already engaged to someone and I didn't want to impose on her. I left it to her to choose me over him, if she felt more strongly for me. I don't think I was as sure of my emotions as she was, hence, I didn't commit anything. She tried to read my emotions, but I wanted her to choose me at her own risk.

She got married to her fiancé and I moved on in my life too. Till then I did not know that we were destined to play much bigger roles in each other's lives.

We accidently met again, eight years later when she was divorced and had a son, and I was married to Neha and had a young daughter.

We magnetically got drawn to each other, maybe owing to the incompleteness we left in each other when we had parted previously. She was very content in her being and she had chosen to move on from her marriage, for she didn't feel loved and cared for in it. She was a good mother and soon she and I started becoming too close. I was never really in love with my wife and was living separately, away from her, when I met Maaya again. My wife and I had a lot of differences but because of our daughter and family pressure, we were trying to make the marriage work. However, when Maaya re-entered my life, I could no more deny myself the love that I saw in her eyes for me and my own need to be with someone who resonated with me.

I decided that I would finally take a stand in my marriage and move on from my wife, so that Maaya and I could be together. I was anyway dragging my relationship with my wife, and that wasn't helping either of us.

Maaya and I found so much completion through each other that for a few months we even forgot that our togetherness wasn't destined to be that way. One day out of the blue, my wife just landed at my place with my daughter and my parents, and they all pushed me to reconsider working out my marriage for the sake of the child involved. I felt so ashamed and trapped in my situation that mentally I started feeling distant from Maaya. I told her that my wife and child had come to live with me, and my family wanted me to work out my marriage.

She silently absorbed the pain and yet told me to make my choices with complete freedom of whatever I wanted. She still stood by me while I was confused and unclear. However, she did sense that I was distancing myself from her because maybe that was the only way I could even try giving my marriage a chance.

One fine day she told me that she was moving to Singapore on a six-month assignment. She had hoped that the time away from her would give me clarity on my life and choices. I knew she was hurt since I had not discussed my dilemma with her and just pushed her away without any fault of hers. I was somehow relieved that I would get enough time to sort myself out.

I can now imagine how difficult it must have been for her but Maaya always does the right thing, even if it's painful for her.

Once she was back, I did return to her telling her that I had decided that I would divorce my wife. Even while we were away, I was always a part of her life and she healed herself only to relieve herself of the pain she felt upon being separated from me. However, she was always compassionate and understanding of my dilemma, my wife's position in my life and so, she left it to me to do what I felt was right.

I was such a coward. I pulled her back, loved her back, gave her hope and then eventually I chickened out again. I couldn't deal with the shame of abandoning my daughter and even though I didn't love my wife, I couldn't justify leaving her either. I don't exactly know what stopped me then but all I can say is that I wasn't brave enough.

I hurt Maaya all over again and this time the damage was irreparable. She left me and maybe even left India forever. I don't know where she has gone. I don't know how she is. I moved to Singapore on the pretext of an official assignment only to look for her. I can't seem to live and breathe without her. I see her everywhere. I can feel her all the time. It's like a shadow that walks with me throughout and yet I cannot touch her. She has made herself inaccessible to me. My craving for her is what led me to start understanding and addressing my inner conflicts.

I know that only Maaya is the one who can fulfil the scarcity of love in my being. She is the embodiment of the goddess and the personification of divine light. However, something keeps me away from her. The more I traverse my journey within, the more I feel it's something in me that cannot allow love and completeness to come to me. As if I am protecting myself against love. I do not know why I would do that but that's what it seems like to me.

I am increasingly becoming resentful of myself. I fail to

understand why I overthink everything. I postpone action. I postpone resolving my life. I postpone making choices. I am waiting for some miracle to happen which will drop her into my lap, though it may yet again end up with her having to go through more despair since my situation still remains where she left me." I felt extremely sad and overwhelmed admitting all of this.

"I can understand that you didn't allow love to come to you. I did that too with Larry. In fact, for several years I felt love is something I can feel but cannot touch. However, you will manage to break this spell if you just keep working on yourself and trust that only love is real," Heather said looking at me.

"Have you now divorced your wife Rahul?" asked Leela.

"No, I have not. I want to but still there is something that does not let me fully take the stand. At some point while living in Singapore, I realized I do not deserve my wife's love too since I am hurting her as well. I know I need to sort myself out, however I am unable to. I also think I crave love and when I get it, I cannot value it," I said.

"Take your time Rahul. Don't rush it this time. Maaya will come to you when you are ready. I can feel it. However, you yet have a lot to recognize within," Gita said to me.

"Yes, I do. She tried to show me all this but at that time I was too egoistic to bother. It is so ironical that today I would give anything to share my spiritual experiences with her but when she wanted to include me on the same path, I mocked her.

I cannot forgive myself for the fact that I used her, loved her, dumped her, betrayed her and abandoned her over and over again but her love for me remained unconditional. She remained just the same. Only her hurt and pain, no matter how hard she hid from me, became more evident with each passing day.

Eventually I think I broke her so badly that she may never be the same Maaya again. I fear meeting her again and I must be resisting it internally, since I do not know what I will do if she tells me that she has moved on and does not share the same connection with me anymore. Perhaps I fear going through what she went through and hence I am more content assuming that wherever she is, she must still love me."

Tears were streaming down my cheeks. I had started to feel helpless and lost all over again. I was unabashed about my thoughts and circumstances in a way I had never been. It sure helped me get more clarity on my inner state.

Being Enough

I want you, I need you, I love you, yet I fear you!
I may not be welcomed,
My past will enter your home with me,
My mistakes will not be forgotten,
My love will be misunderstood,
I might be looked down upon,
Too incomplete I might sound,
I may not be whom you are seeking,
I may not be whom you need after all,
I fear my hope might be destroyed forever,
I think I shall rather live to seek you,

Let me live as if I was enough!
If you accept me nevertheless,
I shall not be able to bear the burden,
My past will then haunt me for being mean and selfish,
On a pedestal I will have to place you,
Love I will make to you but not as an equal,
Forever I might feel I am living with a goddess,
You will see the less I feel in my eyes each day,
The love between us will then be destroyed anyway,
I think I shall rather live to seek you,
Let me live as if I was enough!

Leela put her hand on my right shoulder, as if to reassure me that things would be fine.

"Ok guys, so it's my turn now," said Leela, in a bid to rescue me from all the attention.

"My story is really simple and short. I fell madly in love and married young. We had an amazing life, full of love and laughter for two years. Suddenly my husband started feeling distant from me and one fine day, without giving me any reason whatsoever, he announced that he wanted a divorce.

I am yet to figure out what went wrong because I felt I was a committed and caring wife and lover, and everything was perfect between us.

I came here because the walls of my house haunt me, and I cannot seem to get over him. I am also seeking answers as to what led him to love me and then leave me without even telling me why," saying this Leela had tears in her eyes and she started sobbing again.

Gita and Heather got up to hug her and wipe her tears. “Love has its own ways my dear,” said Heather giving Leela a tight hug.

“Did you have any other relationships after your separation Leela?” enquired Gita.

“Hmmm. Yes, about four of them. However, I am unable to have a committed relationship with anyone since I am still holding on to my ex. No matter how much I try, I keep wondering what was wrong with me or what it was that I failed to do, that pushed him away from me. These questions haunt me,” Leela said with tears continuously flowing.

Gita hugged Leela and patted her on her back.

“I guess you deserve better Leela. Maybe he didn’t dump you. Maybe you chose to move on from him because he couldn’t contain your love in his vessel. I feel you needed a bigger vessel,” Heather said with a certainty in her voice.

Just then Eric arrived with his partner Yami.

Yami and Eric were a gay couple. It was obvious from the way they were holding hands when they met us. We had begun our session a couple of hours prior to when they joined in. Maybe it was their way of getting us acquainted with each other and let the group energy build.

It was a pleasure to see them, for they seemed to be loving and warm people.

Eric was more leader like while Yami looked more emotional or softer of the two.

“You guys must have shared your life stories with each other by now, I hope,” said Eric.

“Yes, we just finished, actually!” I said.

"Great! Let me introduce you to my partner Yami. I told you guys that he would join us later."

Yami said a warm hello to all of us. Eric then introduced us by our names to Yami one by one.

"So, what's your story Eric?" Gita asked curiously.

Eric looked at Yami with a shy smile and said, "Very rarely do people want to know our story. Since you've asked, I would certainly love to share."

He nudged Yami to come with him and they both sat on a rock next to us. We all were sitting in a nice big circle on a rock.

Yami and I met when we were both travelling to Bali from our respective home countries which are Switzerland and Croatia respectively. We instantly clicked since both of us were travelling to forget the heartbreak our previous partners had caused us, and we were perhaps also looking for true love at a deeper level. We then decided to live here in Bali and soon became a part of this organization. We love to work here since the intention here is to help people mend their broken hearts and scarred souls, thus recognizing the infinite source of love they carry within. Our story is as simple as that," he said smiling, turning towards Yami with a look of intense love.

"It's so beautiful that you found what you were seeking in each other. I am so happy for you," said Leela feeling overwhelmed.

"How are you all doing in your inner journey? How have these last few days all by yourself been? Has the food been alright?" Yami enquired.

"The last few days have been intense, even scary to say

the least. However, I can see the point of doing all this. It's so difficult to be alone for so long. For me, the nights have been trying times because my loneliness intensifies. The food is amazing," Leela said.

Eric looked at the rest of us. I couldn't help saying "It has been extremely challenging for me too. My mind doesn't stop thinking and I get tired of dealing with my restlessness, misery and despair which only seem to be increasing. I find myself feeling settled in one moment while extremely anxious in another. So many times, I wonder if I will make it to the last day."

"True. This can happen to most since at a deep level, a lot of us feel lonely and when we are in this kind of a place minus the distractions, the feeling can become overwhelming. Hang in there, you guys!" Eric added.

"Eric, I have had the weirdest experiences in my meditation. I am still trying to understand the message, but I also feel I am touching something relevant about my femininity.

Eric, Yami or any of you guys, please tell me if anyone can explain masculine and feminine aspects within a person with more clarity. I have seen a girl in my visions, during meditation. She said to me that she is my feminine energy. She was extremely sad and grieved. I have been very restless ever since that experience, but I have very limited understanding of this concept.

I would appreciate if anyone could shed some light on this," I requested.

"I think I can explain this one," said Heather and everyone started listening to her attentively.

"Men and women are created differently not because one was meant to rule and the other was meant to serve, but, solely because there are two faculties of the soul's existence as a human being which must always be in balance. It was only natural for them to possess different characteristics. The duality of the physical and the subtle needed to manifest and be understood. This duality formed the basis of gender. Each human being carries both masculine and feminine energies. One's masculine side is that which interacts with the physical world or outside world while one's feminine energy is that which interacts with one's inner world. This is the reason the world has so far functioned such that men naturally took on the roles of taking care of the physicality of things and ensured survival, while women were responsible for nurturing and taking care of the subtle aspects like emotions and relationships.

The male or female body is a representation of the soul's choice of staying more focused on the outer or the inner for the sake of its chosen lessons. As life progressed, the soul created more and more lack of understanding of the inner as the focus on the outer and ensuring survival became primary. It was more important to hunt and fetch food than to feel happy. Worry over survival led to competition, conflicts and there developed inherent lack of trust in the universe and being taken care of, by it. This process put men into a stronger position than women since they were physically stronger. Women were considered weak since they seemed to need men for their survival. Man's need for power over survival then translated into his need to overpower everything including situations, other men, his experiences, his emotions and even women. He started to gain power by suppressing, controlling, abusing his emotions, his inner world as well as the caretaker of that inner world that is his own feminine energy. The value of femininity became so less that women started to be objectified, traded, sold, laid bets upon and violated for display of power by men.

Don't forget while all this was happening, both sides were being lived by the same souls. A soul that chooses to abuse its feminine energy by taking a male's body and abusing women also will then come back as a woman, to be abused at the hands of men.

The soul all this while, was going through a huge inner conflict so that when it took on a human incarnation, the stronger side suppressed or violated the weaker side in its interminable hunger for power.

As the need and chase for power grew, the suppression and torture of femininity also grew. The soul was trapped in it. No matter what gender it chose, it did have to suffer through gender. Sometimes as the oppressor and sometimes as the oppressed, because overall, it was only destroying the self.

However, with time the human mind and consciousness also started recognizing how the experience of power over another person, situation or experience was so shallow. It did realize that the two things it could almost never overpower were, death and the unknown.

This fear of death and the unknown then drew the man to the power of the woman. A woman was less fearful of anything that was not visible. A man could only conquer the visible, but the woman seemed to carry the power to conquer what isn't visible. This intrigued man, since this was an area where he was evidently dependent on the woman. When he was afraid, disappointed, or at loss, he only found solace in the embrace of a woman. She seemed to carry the power to hold him when he was unable to hold himself. She seemed to understand the power of love, of the inner warmth, the spirit.

Slowly with more and more men recognizing their dependency on women, they started to commit to respecting them, loving them and taking care of them in return for being nurtured and being taken care of. This recognition of co-dependency also developed a need to possess a woman else there would be fear of being left alone in imbalance. The woman also needed to be given assurance for her survival. This is when the concept of "Marriage" found its existence.

Marriage was a promise a man and woman made to each other, in the presence of their entire universe (clan), where they vowed to take care of each other being true to their respective characteristics and together, as a unit they would experience harmony and balance. This was also their contribution to the harmony in this universe.

However, slowly as femininity started to be valued by the masculine, it also started to recognize how it had been miserable and in pain all this while. Women started to realize that they had not been given their due in terms of value, respect, love, position, status in the society and they started seeing this as the injustice of men. Women who think so right now, would have also been men at some point enjoying the privileges that the masculine energies enjoyed, including looking down upon women. The men who are being blamed and fought against now could also have lived a past of being abused or violated as women.

This conflict was never that of genders. We have perceived it so. It was of our inability to balance our outer and inner worlds. It is our conflict between the idea of being a soul in a body or a body that has a soul.

Lack of understanding of the relevance of the outer and the inner world and lack of understanding of the role of gender lead us to erroneously believe that we can correct this imbalance by now suppressing, abusing or correcting men. When women do that, they become the masculine within which means they then become whom they are fighting. It is a very simple observation to make. Women who believe feminism is all about fighting against men, start doing to men what they instead claim men have done to women all along. They start behaving like them.

Does this solve the problem? No, it doesn't. The problem only reverses itself. More and more men are feeling like they are being victimized in the name of feminism and equal rights. They are now living what women have lived for eons. The result will be a greater imbalance because we are only jumbling up our own energies and complicating them even more.

This is exactly what is happening inside you Rahul. Your feminine energy needs to be liberated within your own inner world. It is bound, it is feeling suppressed, oppressed and tortured," she said.

I was sad, confused and at loss of words upon hearing

what Heather just shared hence I just nodded signaling acceptance.

"What about homosexual couples like us? What have we chosen Heather?" inquired Eric.

"If you look at yourselves closely Eric and Yami, you'll realize that even though both of you have chosen male bodies, internally Eric has a dominant masculine energy and Yami has a dominant feminine energy. One of you will take care of the outer, which will be you, Eric and one of you will take care of nurturing emotions and the subtle aspects and that will be you, Yami. Irrespective of your choice of body, your inner balance as a couple will still happen through an internal balance of masculine and feminine energies," she answered.

"Wow! Thank you, Heather. This is so amazing. We had never seen it this way. It will take away a lot of conflict from society if we start seeing gender as an internal thing. Thank you for sharing your wisdom. I see it helping me find some answers, personally," said Eric.

"Yes Heather, thank you. I think it makes sense now. I am now beginning to understand the experience I am having within. Maybe when I have it next time, I will be able to help myself gain more inner balance. I just realized that it is possible that my separation from Maaya also is because of my inner separation from my own feminine energy," I said.

"Oh yes, of course! Your inner balance or imbalance between your own feminine and masculine aspects are bound to reflect in your relationships," she confirmed.

"Okay guys, do you mind if I ask you each the meanings

of your names? These are some particularly interesting names and we are extremely curious to understand a connection between your names and your life stories," said Eric.

"We could start with our own. Yami, you go first please."

"'Yami' the twin of Yama. Yama is the lord of death as per Hindu mythology. He takes souls towards the spirit world upon their demise post them releasing their physical bodies. The twin of death is life, however anything that gets associated with death is perceived as dark because death is the least understood and most feared aspect of life.

My father was a scholar who used to study various ancient scriptures and he was guided to name his child Yami. He said that to him, it conveyed transcendence from death, or salvation from the belief that death is an ending. So as per him, unlike the belief of many, Yami represents the inherent light that death carries, which reveals itself as a new form when one dies in their current form," Yami explained.

Everyone clapped to rejoice the new perspective on death.

"I guess we can all see how that name is relevant to your journey. Now it's my turn. 'Eric' means 'the eternal king or emperor' and now that I have heard Yami's definition of his name, I guess I must have some huge connection with Yama, since the lord of death can most convincingly be called the eternal emperor," saying which he smirked.

"Wow," I exclaimed. It was Heather's turn.

"'Heather' is an evergreen flowering plant which even grows on rocks and barren lands. It is also believed to have protective powers. To me my name symbolizes the ability to keep growing and flowering despite encountering barrenness or rocks in my way," Heather said.

Everyone applauded and then looked at Gita.

"'Gita' is derived from the Hindu scripture called the 'Bhagavat Gita' where Gita itself means 'the divine song'. To me it conveys that life is a divine song and like a song, one must sing it to enjoy it. Trying to understand a song too much will take away the joy that one feels from the rhythm, the music, the beats and the words put together. My name reminds me to allow the rhythm rather than analyze life," said Gita.

Listening to the meanings of each one's name was turning into such an engaging and enlightening exercise.

"'Daniel' means 'God is my judge' and I truly believe only the creator knows me wholly and fully. However, it also reveals to me my attachment with judgement, both for self and others. I guess one of my major life lessons in this life is to go beyond judgement. It's the cause for a lot of misery in my life," Dan said.

It was my turn then.

"'Rahul' in Sanskrit means 'able or efficient' and in the Hindu scriptures it's referred to as 'the conqueror of all miseries'. However, I once found an interesting insight into my name. The Egyptian God 'Ra' pronounced as 'Rah' is the Sun God. Rahul derived from 'Rah' is 'the one who is an embodiment of the sun, or who recognizes the light within'. Interestingly, in Sanskrit, 'Raa' means hide or that which is hidden, mysterious or secretive. In Hindu mythology, 'Rahu' is the shadow planet or the planet which hides the truth from one's awareness and keeps them in an 'illusion'. Rahu is said to be in strong opposition with the sun and moon and it casts its shadow to cause solar and lunar eclipses.

While trying to reach a final understanding of my name, I realized that Rahul is the one who destroys the resistance to recognizing the source of light i.e. the sun within, since this resistance creates illusions about life being less than what it should be," saying which I passed the baton on to Leela who was the last in the circle.

Everyone admired my insight into my name.

"'Leela' means 'the divine play' and at this time it totally resonates with my life situation. I guess my journey is to understand the divine play that's going on in my life," she said smiling and looking back at Eric and Yami.

"Phew! This was awesome. Did you guys see how our names are so deeply connected with our journey?" said Eric. Everyone nodded in unison.

We ate, enjoyed some music on a wireless speaker that Yami brought and soon it was time to go back to our respective tents. The sun was about to set, and we had to be in our temporary abodes before dark. "Guys, live well for the next 4 days," said Eric and all of us bid each other goodbye and dispersed to our dens.

The next few days of the retreat passed smoothly with not many dramatic experiences, though I was barely at peace. My heart unceasingly pined for Maaya. My mind constantly told me that she was no more a part of my life and if I continued to be persistent about my chase for a mirage, I would end up losing all I had, for nothing. I dreaded the day when I would be alone and old, with no one next to me. The more my truth became evident to me, the more I realized that I had not only lost Maaya but had even set myself up for losing Neha and Anushka. Even though I was sure I didn't love Neha, I was reminded of the fact that she still loved me and had been trying to make it work between us. I also couldn't help feeling despondent and heartbroken thinking of Anushka and how her life without the constant presence of her father might be. All these thoughts made me feel so crushed that even on a windy evening, I was sweating profusely. Whenever I was frazzled, my palms became sweaty. Maaya had been the one to notice this and ever since, I had started observing this phenomenon too. My palms were soaking wet and I was obviously anxious and muddled in my head.

On the tenth day, though we were still due to meet in another two days, Leela came to my camping site again. She was in bad shape. She seemed to be so frightened that she was trembling. "What happened Leela? Why are you trembling?" I asked her, putting a stole on her shoulders, once I made her sit with me on the ground inside my tent.

She suddenly flung towards me and hugged me tight. "I don't know Rahul. I am so afraid that I will be left alone, and I will die a lonely death. Since the last two nights, I have had vivid dreams of dying alone in a cave, being drowned, being tied in an old building left to rot, dying alone on an island without food and so many more. It's like the moment I close my eyes, these images start coming and I start having palpitations. I wonder what is happening to me. I am so scared that I don't even want to close my eyes," she said.

Upon hearing her I realized her fears were no different

from mine. I too was petrified of how I might end up dying a lonely wretched death. It was not the right time for me to encourage my own fear since I had a situation to handle. I distracted myself from my concerns and brought my focus on Leela, who had been clinging to my chest, sobbing like a child.

"Don't worry Leela," I said running my fingers through her hair and reassuring her that I was there with her. Then I pulled her away from my bare chest and told her that instead of sleeping we could both talk about our lives with each other.

Hearing this, she looked relieved.

Once she was calmer and had taken a few sips of water, I made place for her to sit in my tent. I also quickly pulled out a white t-shirt from my bag and wore it, to avoid feeling awkward. I usually slept bare chested otherwise.

"Leela, would you tell me about your childhood and your family?" I asked her.

A moment of thought later, she shared "I come from a conventional Greek family settled in an old but very beautiful town of Cyprus called 'Othomos' which is very ethnic and set in the mountains. It is close to Limassol.

We Greeks, we put family before everything else. Our lives are all about love, togetherness, parties, food, wine and fun. We enjoy big extended families where kids, cousins, parents, grandparents and everyone is a part of each other's daily lives. Kids can leave and stay separately when they grow older, but they always remain children for their family and are always treated that way. The women enjoy being the authority figure at home while the men fulfil their responsibilities well by ensuring financial stability and protection of the family.

We are light-hearted people who believe in simple lives where as long as the food, booze and merry making goes on, life is good. In our family, I remember when I was a kid, every Friday evening onwards the entire weekend was a celebration. My mother and my aunts used to cook Makaronia tou fournou and my dad and uncles used to set up their barbeques. All the kids of the family were left together in one big house with a courtyard where they could play, fight or do whatever they liked. Every weekend was like one big picnic and we all collectively just enjoyed life.

In my culture, breaking a family that too, without giving a genuine reason is considered to be a sin. My parents are still shocked at Simon's decision. They can't understand why a man would want to leave his wife because they come from a town where this is unheard of.

I have been brought up with so many siblings and cousins in such a protected and happy environment that dealing with this loneliness now is getting to me. I had never ever imagined that a day would come when I would have to live without my husband, all by myself.

Even though I am well acquainted with the world, my thought process is still very conventional. I had imagined taking care of him, having many children, enjoying a life filled with love, food and drinks. In Greek, there is a saying "Ou theos na mas ie vlebi" which means "God protect us," and I really lived by it.

"I understand. How are Greek men? Are they dominating at home?"

"They are the providers, thus proud of themselves but they also make caring husbands and fathers, always instilling traditional Greek values and morals in the children whilst being there to support them and care for them. They like to hold their head high and don't want to be seen as weak or soft, but they are gentle at heart," she said.

"What stops you from believing that you will find love again, Leela? You are a beautiful, loving and generous girl. Do you realize how miserable your life would have been if Simon would have chosen to stick around for the sake of family values or culture without any love in his heart? Isn't a heartbreak once and for all better than getting your heart broken every single day?" I tried to reason with her.

"I agree Rahul and I do understand this. I also understand that if his love for me was over, then what he did was the right thing. It's just that I am unable to believe that such a thing could happen, that his love could vanish just like that," she said before she had started sobbing again.

Whenever I saw Leela's inability to believe that her husband had abandoned her, my thoughts went to Maaya. I secretly asked God for forgiveness. It was through Leela's misery and despair that I realized how much agony I had given Maaya, and yet she was graceful enough to never blame me for it.

I wish I knew...

I never knew you would leave my hand,
I never knew you would walk alone,
I never knew I would be on my own,

I never knew myself other than with you.
I never knew how painful it would get,
I never knew I would no more sleep,
I never knew the hurt will stay forever,
I never knew it would scar my soul.
I wish I knew you'd leave me,
I wish I knew we never belonged together,
I would have then held myself back,
I would have never loved you more than myself,
I would have never let you know how much I loved you,
I would have never walked with you on those starry nights,
I would have never let you hold me,
I would have never let you tell what you told me,
I would have left you before you left me,
I would have done to you what you did to me,
Oh Lord! Now I realize,
Aren't you I am?
Only disguised as me!

Somehow, in that moment a very profound realization occurred to me. At some level, we are all equally capable of love and abandon both. It's just that when someone else gives us the experience which was not a reciprocation of our choice of love or abandon, we feel deceived. However, if we were in their situation, we know deep down that we would have done exactly what they did to us.

"Leela, let's accept that he is not coming back ever

again. Good or bad, he was whom you loved. Is it wise to keep holding on to why or how he did what he did? Are you not still holding on to him through your disbelief?" I enquired.

She suddenly started crying even more and pulled herself closer to me to hug me. I was wearing a thin white t-shirt and as she snuggled, her cheek touched the bare skin on my chest, and I could feel her warm breath. I tried to calm her down, though I was also awkward in the way she was holding me. Since I knew she was feeling very helpless, I did not find it appropriate to pull away just yet.

For a faint moment, I felt as though Leela softly kissed my chest. She was still holding me tight and my hands were also wrapped around her back, holding her against my chest. Her breasts were squeezed against me in a tight hug and her breath was getting heavier. She was like a butterfly yearning for a cocoon, to feel safe and protected within its walls. We stayed like that for a while and honestly, it felt comforting to have someone to hold and cuddle. She was extremely scared and so was I because at some level we shared a common fear...that of a lonely ending.

Soon, I pulled her away from my chest and looked at her in the eye. "Leela, I can understand that you are feeling vulnerable right now and are looking to me for support. I will always be there to support you, as a friend."

She nodded, with her eyes becoming extremely heavy. She had been too exhausted and worn out with the continuous crying. I let her lie down in my tent on one side and spread the extra sheet I had, over her. I decided to meditate. It was a full moon night and I couldn't lose the chance to experience higher and more conducive energies.

I went out quietly and sat on the rock. It was pitch dark with only the moon leaving its reflection over the lake, making everything appear so much more beautiful and divine. I closed my eyes soaking in the serenity and allowed myself to travel as far as I could, within.

It didn't take me long to reach her, yet again. Even before I reached her, her sobs reached me, which guided me to her. I started to feel the familiar sinking sensation. Strongly pulled towards her, I could finally see her. She was still sitting in the same posture with her head cupped in her knees, crying profusely.

I bowed down and touched her shoulder again. Why are you crying so much? I asked her. She gently raised her head and looked at me with her teal eyes glistening with tears. "I am very lonely here," she responded. "Who left you here?" I asked further.

"You," she responded.

This is where we left off last time. I was keen to understand her further. Just then I heard a hiss. It was scary. The chill in the place was increasing. She started squeaking and held me tight, as if looking for guarding herself from someone. She was looking in a direction, where all I could see was absolute darkness. Her hands and body were trembling, and I also started to feel as if there was someone there, but I couldn't see who.

Slowly, I heard a voice. "Hmmmm. I see. You are here after all?" said a very loud demonic voice.

In the direction from where the voice was coming, I started to see an opening. We were inside a dark cave while on the other side of it there was not only darkness but also the sky. I thought I started to see the silhouette of a creature. It wasn't entirely a big bird or a dragon, neither was it a death-eater, but it was something of the sorts. All I could see were two piercing red eyes which were huge and fierce. The fear I felt left me frozen.

With all the courage I could muster, I managed to utter, "Who are you?"

"I am your wisdom. I am here to give you some of what I have," he said and then he twirled around in his position to give me a complete look at how humongous he was. Eventually he faced us again from the little opening of the cave. It seemed to me that he was too big to enter the place we were in; hence he could only talk to us from a distance. This recognition alone brought me some relief. This is when my attention went to what he had just said.

"My wisdom?"

That sounded so bizarre.

"I know you don't believe me when I say I am your wisdom. Trust me, I find myself equally misplaced. Once upon a time, I was angelic. I used to fly in the skies and when my pristine white wings touched the air, they would begin to shower glitter from the sky. My touch was the touch of God and anything that I held, illuminated like gold. I emanated golden light, spreading love and divinity everywhere I went," he said with his voice trailing into a deep pain and sadness as he finished.

"How come you started looking like this then? Who did this to you?" I inquired.

"You. It all happened because of you," he said in a loud roar that shook me off balance and had me fall flat on the ground.

"Me?" I trembled.

"Yes. You!"

"You have been careless, reckless and extremely insensitive to me. You have never valued my guidance. You have for long held on to your self-perceived image. It serves you since it helps you stay delusional about life and your chosen lessons. It serves you because it allows you to believe you are in control. The more you fed your ego, the darker I became. My wings started to lose their power. My flight started to lose its heights. No more glitter and no more sparkle, for my throne was taken away by your ego. You have always chosen to deny the truth and believe in what gives you power and control over others. The golden heart you were born with has been slowly captured and now it's your ego's kingdom that I live in. Helpless and distraught, I must succumb to these dark and dense times," he said.

I could make no sense of this conversation, but I could undoubtedly feel he was deeply wounded.

Just then my attention went to her. "Why do you scare her? What has she done?" I asked in a slow and polite tone, making sure I didn't flare him up once more.

"I don't mean to scare her. I just want to take her from here. She refuses to go with me. She still has hope from you. I want her to see the truth. She still waits for you to salvage her. She still thinks one day, you will embrace her and reclaim your golden throne. She does not realize how powerful your ego has become. Now nothing can stop it. Honestly, I want her to come with me and just give up on you, the way I have. I know you will suffer for your ego will guzzle you. That wicked one, it spares none.

I reckon that will be the right punishment for you. I want you to suffer. She and I will perish in this dark world anyway. Wherever we stay, we will only die bit by bit. I have accepted that my fate is to embrace this darkness, but I fail to understand her optimism. I want her to see that what she hopes for, is never going to happen.

You must ask her to come with me. Look how frail she has become. I will feed her and give her company till these clouds of your ignorance consume us. If your ego finds her before me, she will be brutally killed, and her innocence shall be mutilated. I want her to depart with grace. "

I was so aghast upon hearing this. It was shameful. I was completely oblivious to the happenings inside myself. The thought that it was causing misery and hurt to someone was distressing.

With a jerk, I was pushed out of my experience straight into the consciousness of my surroundings. I couldn't see anything for a few seconds; all my senses felt numb. In a while I registered that something happened within me, during my meditation. It was so surreal that it had jolted me completely.

There was a deep sense of loss and a void in my

heart. I didn't know how to interpret these encounters in my meditation. The sheer intensity of them made me conjecture that they were significant. I was not sure anyone else would believe me if I shared them.

I looked up at the sky, which suddenly seemed so dark. I wanted to scream out at God or the angels or whoever would hear me. Why was this happening to me? What had I done? Was I such a bad person on the inside? I wanted to cry, to just unburden myself of all my anguish. I had so patiently trodden the long and lonely road to self-recognition but this self that I was being revealed was not what I was hoping to discover. I always thought of myself as an authentic person who was morally upright enough to choose a rotten marriage over separation from his wife, for the sake of his young child. What was so wrong in what I had done? All these visions, however made me feel devilish. As if I was this wretched being who had hurt people for my own selfish needs. All of this was difficult to believe or accept and yet, all of these experiences were stemming from within me. Since no other was showing it all to me, there was hardly a way to deny them either. They were taking a toll on my self-esteem. I couldn't sleep that night. I made sure I tossed and turned carefully since I didn't want to disturb Leela's sleep. My nature, my character, my choices, my expression and my very being had become questionable. I was so worn out by the millions of thoughts that cluttered my mind that it was in the wee hours that I finally managed to fall asleep.

Leela had left by the time I woke up. I assumed she

was feeling better and had probably left for her own early morning routine. I was glad she had gone. I was too flustered myself, to be of any help to her. I wanted to stay in my shell for a while to make sense of myself and the revelations. At the same time, she needed to learn to trust herself and deal with her weak moments.

Just then, it occurred to me that perhaps Heather could help me. I made a mental note to seek her opinion on the experience I had the previous night, when we all met next, which was on the twelfth day, just one day away.

Meanwhile, I wrote my experience so that I could capture the essence to explain to Heather when I would go to seek her guidance.

That evening was calm and serene. I had put aside my thoughts in some deep forbidden recess of my mind, to be retrieved later. To distract myself, I did some yoga during the day and just sat on the rock admiring the sunset and then appreciating the emerging moon. I realized I had resistance to going within and invoking that experience again, so I decided not to meditate and just let things be till I got further insight. At night, I woke up twice, feeling extremely hot and sweaty as if I was experiencing hot flashes. The night passed again in anxiousness, tossing and turning to get some sleep.

Finally, another day arrived when all of us had to gather together. I always looked forward to our meeting, since it was insightful and enriching to get to know each life from so many different perspectives. Each time, I came back feeling more in love and gratitude for life. This time though, I was just grateful for some company. It was tough to be all by myself anymore with my inner adventures that left me feeling drained and lost.

We all met again. I got an opportunity to talk to Heather alone and I shared with her all that was happening in my meditations. She seemed astonished. Perhaps she knew what was happening. She took my hand lovingly between both her palms, closed her eyes and stayed like that for a while, as if in deeper prayer. Upon opening her eyes after a few moments, she offered me some water to drink. She pulled out a tiny Buddha figurine made of limestone from her bag and pressed it in my palm.

"Rahul keep this in your hand, when you meditate next. Additionally, bring this acceptance deep within that you forgive yourself for your ways and for being ignorant of what you were doing to yourself. The next time you have the vision, just sit there next to the girl, even if she is crying. Look into her eyes and hold her hands. Reassure her of your presence and let her know that you have realized her worth. Build a love-based relationship with your feminine counterpart within and the more you do that, the more you will experience changes in your entire inner experience. Be sure that your emotion must be extremely genuine and from the depth of your heart. This Buddha will help you stay grounded and face your innermost truth. Don't worry honey, it may all seem weird and scary but it's all good. You are only coming out of the worst. Just allow it to come through," she said as she stood up to lovingly hug me.

Her embrace was so full of love and her heart was so

open that I could feel the energy of love travelling from her into my heart chakra. It was so reassuring. Her embrace was almost maternal. Through the retreat I had come to realize that some people are so compassionate that just by being in their presence, love and peace can be felt. I secretly hoped to become like her someday. I acknowledged her going through a fair share of experiences, to become who she was to me that day.

I never had the encounter again with my feminine energy up until the eighteenth day. I had mentally prepared myself to face whatever that was within me. I had been having conversations within myself where I accepted that I had failed to understand this aspect of my being so far, but I was ready. I was ready to accept the sensitive, thoughtful, emotional side of me. I was ready to acknowledge everything I did only to satisfy my male ego and seek forgiveness for the same.

Heather had given me a book to read, which explained the ego rather interestingly. It also explained how one's ego develops an identity of its own within one's mind, if it's not brought to awareness. The book was extremely relatable, and it included deep insights into how the root of all ego was fear. It helped me identify my core fears which led me to create a defense around myself, thus creating my ego. It said that behind the mighty ego lied an extremely fearful, meek and defenseless being who was using the ego as a shield to protect himself from his own truth. When I thought of it, it made sense. Whenever someone is shown their fear or weakness, their ego takes over and they react in unpredictable and mostly unforgiving ways.

When I thought about my own ego, at first it was tough to understand. Then using a theory given in the book, I was able to recognize my deepest fears. One of my deepest fear was of "being disrespected by society" and I guess this played a huge role in why I couldn't take a stand to leave my marriage and be with Maaya. The ego I thus created was that "I am sacrificing love to save my marriage."

I had slowly started to realize how in the trap of my ego, I had been unfair to Maaya, to Neha, to my parents and my child. I had created a whole self-image where I was the one who was just, authentic and genuine. I did everything to suppress or remove whatever appeared to be challenging my right, calling it wrong. I had failed to understand my roles. I got rid of people and relationships to stay in a safe zone where I only experienced what I wanted to; however, it was likeable to me. I lived life avoiding conflicts. I dreaded facing conflicts. To avoid them, I chose to avoid those people, relationships or situations who brought me face to face with my conflicts.

Through Maaya, I faced my biggest conflict. My entire sense of identity was at stake. To accept Maaya and let go of my marriage, I ought to embrace being wrong. I was to own up to having failed my marriage and my family. This failure further revealed that I made the wrong choices. Being wrong was in conflict with my self-image. I found it easier to correct it all by moving away from Maaya. That was the shortest solution to becoming "right" again. I was sure I would be able to convince myself someday that in fact all was right, and it was only me who couldn't see it thus far. However, even though I did disconnect with Maaya and had hurt her so much, my wrong remained wrong. It rather exposed more wrong in several other aspects of my life. My relationship with my parents had turned sour because they neither understood my fascination with Maaya nor resonated with my lack of sensitivity towards my wife and child. My work was affected because I couldn't focus on it as it seemed purposeless. When I asked myself why I wanted to achieve well at work or in life, there was no answer. Everything was becoming meaningless and I was getting trapped in the meaningless existence that I was becoming.

Ever since Heather had given me the Buddha, something had shifted within me. I was becoming more responsive to my self- awareness. For the first time, I could feel my self-talk revealing aspects of myself which I had so far shut off for the fear of being judged.

On that day when I sat for the meditation, I almost knew that I was ready to have an encounter with him and with her and it was destined to be something substantial. The feeling was so intense that rather than questioning it, I just allowed it to take me further. I sat on the rock, which was my favorite place to meditate, just before sunset. The sunset always drew my attention. That was the most beautiful sunset I had ever seen. The hues in the sky were surreal. I was already in a trance by just witnessing it. As soon as it began to get dark, I closed my eyes.

Within what felt like a few moments, I was travelling down the various tunnels to where she was. This time, I reached the same place but there was no one there. It was pitch dark. She was missing. A sinking feeling took over as I wondered if she had finally given up and gone with the beast. The thought was scary and yet I knew it was a possibility. I soon searched for that opening from where I saw the dark energy who called himself my "wisdom." It was there. I decided to step onto the other side. For a moment, I was frightened and unsure. What if I could never come back? What if it was just a trap? What if, I would be lost forever? This time though, I was determined to go all the way. I remembered what Heather had said. The Buddha would protect me, thinking of whom, I stepped outside the cave into a new dimension.

It was a different world out there. The sky was grey, as if it was about to rain. It was cold, like in winter. There was snow all around. There was an eerie chill created by absolute silence. Dry trees with no leaves and lots of snow deposited on them overwhelmed the landscape. There was no one, absolutely no one in sight. I didn't even know whom to call out to. I was also afraid of the beast catching up with me before I could reach her. Zillions of thoughts crisscrossed my mind and the deathly chill was not helping. I was in Narnia all by myself and I didn't know what to do. Eventually when the cold was getting to me, I decided to go back to the cave.

The moment I stepped back, there was some sort of movement around me. I couldn't say what it was, but it seemed like something had moved. I kept moving towards the cave, freezing every second.

Suddenly I saw him, standing right opposite me. His darkness was appalling. He was like a shred of a dark cloud itself with eyes to see, ears to listen and a mouth to speak with. I couldn't completely say if it was a shadow, a cloud or a being. Somehow, even though all this while I feared encountering him, now that he was there, I was scared no more. The cold was distracting me, but I attempted to focus on what he had to say.

"Finally, you arrive," he said in his husky voice.

"Yes! I am here. Where is she? Is she ok?" I enquired, wondering why she wasn't with him.

"Don't worry I wouldn't do anything to her. She is as much a part of me as she is of you," he said.

I suddenly sensed that he was mellowing down. He didn't seem as upset with me as he had been the last time we met.

"What are you here for?" he asked me before I could finish contemplating my thoughts.

"I want to talk to her. I just want to hold her. I want to make sure she is fine. I want to explain myself. I didn't hurt any of you on purpose. I just don't know what is happening. I want to help," I blurted out.

"Why do we matter? Why does she matter?" he retorted.

"I don't know. I feel for her. I feel she and I are the same person in some way. I can feel her pain in my heart. I don't understand this connection but whenever I have seen her crying, I have felt responsible. Even you said I was responsible. I want to relieve her of her pain. I want to make her feel loved and accepted. I don't even know how that can happen but that's how I feel," I said.

"Do you see the barrenness in this land? Can you feel the chill here? Do you hear the haunting silence here? Do you know what this is?" he retorted, and I could feel his energy was getting anxious and restless now.

I looked around saying "Yes, I can feel it all. I don't know what place this is though."

"This is the place of creation of love inside your heart," to my surprise the beast said.

I was zapped. If this was where love was to be created in my heart, how come it was so empty, chilly and lifeless?

"Exactly! This lifelessness is your doing," he said. That's when I realized, he could read my thoughts.

"How can you read my thoughts? Who are you?" I said

"I am your wisdom, Rahul. Remember?" he said.

Though I could recall him telling me this earlier, I still couldn't believe him. Brushing away those thoughts, I carried on the conversation.

"Can I meet her? I don't understand what you say but let me please see her. I want to comfort her."

"She is not here. She has been taken away by Chazaq. He has held her captive," he announced.

I suddenly felt my blood rushing and a certain panic arose in me.

"What do you mean? Who is Chazaq? Why would he capture her? Where are they?" I asked him.

"Huh!" he exclaimed before swirling around and swiftly moving away from me, dismissing my concerns.

"Hey Mr. Wisdom, please stop. Please tell me how I can reach her?" I pleaded to him.

He swirled around in a quick, swift movement, anguished, as if I had offended him. "My name is Aaron and she is Sarah. You better use our names when you address us," he yelled.

"Ok, sure. I am sorry Aaron. Please help me find Sarah. I must see her. I must help her," I pleaded.

"I don't know if you are capable of doing what you intend to do. I don't know if you realize the difficulty of what you want to do. I don't even know if I can trust you and tell you the whole story," he said now sounding helpless.

I was down on my knees. Something inside me was making me desperate to seek his help. "Please trust me Aaron. If you say all this is my doing, then for sure I should be the one to rectify it. Please guide me just this one more time. I know I may have let you down but this time, I am determined to bring closure to all that isn't serving me and restore peace and love in my heart. I request you to tell me how my heart became the way it looks now. Why is everything here so cold, so empty, so chilly and so frozen? What has happened here?"

He seemed to melt slowly. "Hmmm. Okay. Let me help you one more time. It is my nature to guide so I cannot refuse guidance when sought by you. Helping you reach your next stage is my role to play. Alright then! I will share with you the entire story and then I will leave."

"Thank you."

"This was a beautiful place to dwell. Your heart was full of love, kindness, purity and compassion. You treated everyone well and loved yourself too. Sarah was the queen of your heart and she was fair and kind. I was her confidante and guide. Whenever there was a matter that triggered a conflict in your heart, Sarah sought guidance from me, and you counselled with her to resolve it. Together you and she were one within. Whatever arose to disturb the balance of your heart, your acceptance and oneness with her, coupled with my guidance was able to restore love and peace in this kingdom. But then, Maaya happened!" saying which he stopped.

"Maaya? What about her? What do you know about her?" I asked.

"I know everything about her and you. I have known her for several lifetimes. She has been with you through ages. Her presence in your life blossomed your heart. Her love for you inspired you to create more love for yourself and others. You became a better person and your heart emanated compassion. Those were the days when my wings shone in a golden aura and Sarah would sing and dance all day since the happier you were, the more you cared for her too. She, after all, is your own feminine aspect, the completion with whom you lived through Maaya and vice versa," he said.

"Really? How does that work? Where did all that happiness go then? Why couldn't I contain that love and happiness?"

"Chazaq! He took it all away." He responded, sounding grieved.

"Who is Chazaq? How could he take away my happiness and love from my heart?" I was curious.

"He is your ego, Rahul. Your ego took away everything from you. He ruined it all. He sucked out the beauty from your heart and made it empty and barren," Aaron said.

"Hmmmm. What is the connection between Chazaq and Maaya?" I asked, trying to understand the bigger picture here.

"Maaya loved you from the depth of her soul. She gave you so much unconditional acceptance that you dwell in pride within. You forgot that her ability to love reflected who she was. You were to stay in gratitude for her being there. You instead started to believe you were perhaps too deserving of that kind of love and hence Chazaq became powerful. He always existed, even in the days when all was green and beautiful here. In those days however, he remained in his own area where he created a peaceful dwelling. He was content with whatever he had and was never seeking more. We had a happy co-existence with him. However, when you started taking Maaya's love for granted, he started to get energized and more powerful. He stopped listening to us and he stopped following Sarah's bidding. He started to claim a bigger share of your heart and our space started to squeeze in. We did call out to you, but you couldn't hear us since Chazaq was able to reach out to you sooner and faster. He thrived on your fears and those, you had many. You were smitten by his might and his powers since he allowed you to hide from your fears. He made you feel you are the God of love and you can create an inner experience of exhilaration and completeness whenever you want. You started to lose recognition of Maaya's contribution to the beauty you lived within. Chazaq was sure he couldn't allow Maaya to stay in your life much longer since the more she loved you, the weaker he became. He thus did the unfathomable. He sent out vibrations from your heart to attract Neha and Anushka back into your life," I heard.

The ground under my feet seemed to be sinking with this narration. The silence was getting deeper. I was bewildered at all that was going on; I was now wondering whether this was beyond the grasp of my awareness or was it that I had deliberately chosen to stay oblivious. Now, this was my concern.

"Why don't I feel the same way for Neha, the way I feel for Maaya? Why couldn't her presence blossom my heart?" I asked Aaron.

"Well, for that you will need to understand your own past. You have lived several lives with Neha in different roles, and with Maaya too. You have a deep connection with both. However, their roles in your current life are different. You have chosen to recognize oneness between your masculine and your feminine aspects within, as a part of your life lessons in this lifetime. To be able to do that, you needed someone who would give you the taste of that oneness and how beautiful it feels when your heart is full of love. You also needed someone who takes away that oneness and shows you how ugly it can be without love in your heart. You have chosen Maaya to be the one who shows you your inner beauty while Neha as the one who reveals to you your inner lack of beauty. Without knowing how it feels to be devoid of something, one cannot appreciate or value it. The roles that either of them plays, says nothing about them but only about your past with them. When for a certain lesson or a certain type of experience is needed, there is a place that's created in our lives for that role. Then a soul who has a karmic past that can justify that role, is invited to participate in it. For the role of fulfilling your inner void with love and revealing to you the beauty of love, you could only invite a soul that carried so much love for you that enabled you to manifest such an experience. Your karmic history with Maaya is such that she did carry the unfulfilled desire to love you more than herself. It came from some lifetime in which she had to abandon you but could never forgive herself for having done so. Hence, she was a suitor for that role," he revealed.

After a moment of contemplation, "What about Neha? Why was she chosen?" I wanted to know.

"For the role where she will empty you of love and reveal to you your ego, only a soul who could touch and wound your ego was needed. Ego is like a defense one creates to project themselves as being immune to hurt and failure. A soul that you have failed or hurt in the past was the most suitable one to take on this position because it's easy to project strength in front of the one who is unaware of your inner vulnerability but those who can make you vulnerable and guilty cannot be escaped from. Chances are that when you meet a soul whom you have hurt or failed in the past, you will develop defenses to ensure they don't recognize you or expose you. This barrier between you and them also never allows the love inside to blossom, hence revealing the ego. Neha was such a soul whom you had failed and hurt in two lifetimes where you couldn't take responsibility for her, once as a parent and another as a husband. She was hence perfect to reveal your inability to nurture another and your tendency to escape the situation whenever faced with your ego," Aaron explained.

I felt I could finally understand something. As if what he was telling me connected the dots. I had beaten myself up for way too long wondering what was wrong with Neha that I couldn't love her or feel for her the way I did for Maaya. Understanding that they had different roles to play in my life lifted some part of the burden and made it easier for me to accept my truth.

"Aaron, now I am realizing all this. Had I not been understanding that I have gone wrong, I wouldn't be here talking to you. I am transforming. Why is it that now Chazaq holds Sarah captive? Isn't this transformation good?" I asked.

"You don't get it, do you? He said as he sneered. The transformation is good for you but not good for Chazaq. You are not your ego Rahul. Just get that! Chazaq, who is your ego separates you from me. He also separates you from Sarah, who is your inner feminine. Chazaq becomes weak if this transformation goes on this way, he fears he will fail. Ever since our last meeting, Sarah had started to feel better. She had started to harbor the hope that eventually you would come around and come out of Chazaq's spell. When he found this out, he was insecure. He immediately held her captive. I have become much weaker than I was. I don't have much power over him. I couldn't save her. This is exactly why I wanted Sarah to come with me the other day. I feared Chazaq might do this, but I am not heard in these times anymore. There was a time my word was valued as the word of God. Now I find myself becoming a mere witness to the growing powers of Chazaq and the deteriorating rein of Sarah," he said.

"Aaron, I am sorry I have disappointed you. How can I empower you? Tell me," I asked.

"I don't think you can empower me anymore Rahul. That stage is gone. I am fading away. My times are over. I have served you in bringing you to this stage. It's now time for renewed wisdom to arise inside you. That will happen when you are able to dissolve Chazaq into nothingness and rescue Sarah. I don't know how that will happen and how you will reach him. No one knows where Chazaq comes from and where he disappears to. I guess you will know when you are ready to face him. For now, you must leave. I am frail and tired; I can help you no more!" saying which he swiftly flipped and disappeared.

I started to feel the chill and haunting silence again. I slowly moved back to the cave and soon found myself on the rock, back with a jerk in my body that threw me off balance and I fell sideways on the grass.

When I opened my eyes, for a few seconds, I could not make sense of anything. It was as though I was in another era, another space, another time. I wasn't sure whether I was meditating or dreaming or what exactly was happening. I couldn't quite recall my entire experience too, except that I remembered I had to rescue someone and fight someone. I felt so exhausted as if a lot of time had passed. When I saw my watch, I was shocked. Coincidently I had checked the time just before closing my eyes. Exactly two minutes had passed since then. I couldn't believe I had lived an entire era within a span of two minutes. It was unbelievable. I had once read somewhere that sometimes when we experience our inner reality, no physical time lapses during that experience because we enter a dimension where time does not exist. This was my first experience where this did indeed appear to be true. I was very overwhelmed not just by the experience but also by the time. I didn't feel like eating dinner, so I just went to sleep. That night I slept like a log.

Soon the retreat came to an end. We all met each other after packing up our belongings on the last day, to tread back to the organizer's office. We exchanged greetings and our contact details, hugged each other goodbye and then travelled to Singapore. I rushed to the airport to catch the evening flight back home. The others either stayed on in Bali a little longer or had flights the following morning.

Someone tapped on my shoulder and as I woke up, an extremely beautiful air hostess asked me, "Sir, do you want me to get more wine for you? Or something to nibble?"

I thanked her politely, but I didn't want to drink more since I realized it was hitting me a bit too quickly. Maybe since I had been off drinks for 3 weeks and after doing so much inner work, my capacity to consume alcohol was impaired.

Those 21 days were intense, profound and yet exhausting. I needed at least a day or two of complete rest and assimilation time in my own space to become ready to go to work. I had intentionally scheduled my return on Friday evening so that by Monday morning, I would be ready to get back to the grind.

It was extremely relaxing to be back in my apartment. Once my flight from Bali took off, I had shut down the doors of my mind, intending to view everything with a fresh perspective once I was well rested at home. Upon reaching home, I slept for twelve hours straight, and woke up feeling rejuvenated.

□

Back Home

Everything about my life felt new after I came back from the retreat. I felt so much at peace with myself. I didn't feel the need to rush things, to prove myself, to struggle, to slog or to work late nights. I felt like cooking my own meals rather than ordering in. I loved spending time all by myself just reading a book or maybe watching a good movie. I was less guilty while talking to Anushka and keeping the phone down without feeling obligated to talk to Neha too. When I thought of Maaya, there was a renewed sense of love for her. I no longer found faults in myself to justify the lack of her presence in my life, neither did I glorify her for who she was. I was just happy to feel her as a part of me. This happiness though, also then translated into a deep sense of loss when I recognized that I had perhaps lost her forever. Ever since I had returned, my insane chase for Maaya had softened and perhaps the acceptance of having lost her forever was settling in.

I started to talk much lesser and kept to myself. The time I spent with myself was peaceful, if the thought of Maaya not being there didn't cross my mind. Once it did, a gloom seeped in. This time it was without the guilt and the blame, just simple sadness.

Surprisingly, even though I was not really chasing any targets, things were falling in place and I was able to afford my relaxation time without losing out on my performance at work, which was amazing. I often thought about those profound experiences I had while I was meditating. Even though there was a sense of incompletion to them, those experiences never happened to me again, ever since I had returned.

Dan contacted me about two weeks later. He wanted to go out for coffee. I agreed, and we met on a Thursday evening at a Starbucks outlet near our workplace. I was due to go back to India in another couple of weeks since my assignment in Singapore was coming to an end. I was slightly disappointed because I had failed to find Maaya. However, I was also glad that I was going to go back home transformed. I had decided that my priority was to resolve my own life and relationships without which even if Maaya came into my life again, I would not be able to give her the life she deserved. There was some satisfaction for having received some clarity about the direction I was meant to take. While I waited for Dan at the coffee shop, I imagined how my mum and dad would feel when I would pay them a surprise visit in Bangalore before going back to Delhi. The last time I saw my parents had been over two years ago and I was sure they would be happy. I had lots to catch up with them since when they came with Neha and Anushka, insisting that I reconcile with my wife to save my marriage.

Dan and I had a conversation where we tried to understand how we had moved forward in our lives post the retreat. Dan asked me if I could collect some *"raakh"* (ashes) from a certain place in Bangalore. The place seemed to be close to my parents' house, but upon enquiring about the purpose, he just dared me saying, "I bet you are scared but if you have the courage, do it man." He said he needed it as a part of a ritual he was doing with a guy for his spiritual practices.

Two weeks went by quickly and I was soon at my parent's place in Bangalore. My parents were elated to see me. My mother served me tea and snacks with moist eyes.

The evening I landed, I was too tired, so I went to sleep early. The following day, we spent a lot of time together where we talked about my life, my work and I shared with them everything that had happened to me in the last two years without filtering out details. I wanted them to be clear about my state of mind. They listened to me patiently and many times my mother looked at my father while I talked about how lost and confused about my life I had been, and my father kept giving her a reassuring look, as if to say that I would find my way out of my mess.

For me, being able to open myself up to them and just speaking my heart out was in itself, a healing process.

As requested by Dan, I was to collect the *raakh* from a place near my home. I didn't know anyone there and I didn't know how to approach this, so I shared the request with my mother.

She somehow was visibly shocked.

Initially she discouraged me saying I should stay away from this kind of stuff.

"You hardly understand what goes around in such

kinds of places," she said. I didn't budge because I didn't want Dan to think I couldn't do a simple thing for him. He had given me the address of the place, requesting my help. "I must go there, and I am not bothered about whatever goes on there. It's just that I don't know how to enter the place if they won't allow me to," I said to my mother.

My mother asked me to go to sleep promising me that she would find a way. The next afternoon, we happened to be crossing that place. My father was driving the car and as we approached the gate of the building where we were to go, my mother asked him to park on the opposite side of the road for a few minutes under the pretext that I had some stuff to pick from there. He agreed since he also had some errands to run in the market nearby. My mother and I got off the car and crossed the road.

"Mom, I can do this by myself. You don't need to go there," I told her. She simply held my hand and pulled me closer to the place saying, "You don't know how to handle these people Rahul. I will talk to them. It's difficult to enter such places because these people at the entrance are very wary of whom they allow inside. You won't be allowed to enter the way you think. Come, let me help you. I have this bag with me. We can procure what you want and quickly leave," she said.

Understanding her concern as a mother, I agreed. As we reached the entrance of the big blue gate, the person at the entrance refused to let us in. My mother explained to him the purpose of our visit and asked him to help us out. He refused to budge until she slipped him a hundred rupee note.

He saw the money and immediately grabbed it from my mother before anyone saw it. Then he said, "Please be quick. It's not a good idea to stay too long. You seem to be here for the first time. Just do whatever you must and quickly move out."

"Thank you," she said, pulling me along towards the building in the middle of the huge plot. The entrance of the building was hidden behind lots of rags hanging from the top of the ceiling as if to camouflage the entry. As we approached the entry, she removed one of the rags hanging vertically from the ceiling, by the hand, revealing the doorway through which we entered. As we entered, I realized the place inside was a big courtyard like area where many people were sitting. Some of them were praying with their eyes closed while others were just sitting and looking ahead where a few people huddled together were speaking to each other. It was a particularly unimpressive and dimly lit place. The tin roof of the courtyard also blocked any natural light of the day, which only seemed to break through its tattered and jagged edges. My mother then held my hand and looked at me, saying "Rahul, I will go and get you the *raakh* in this bag. You must just stand here and watch. You just have to assure me of one thing, my son."

"What?" I said. "No matter what happens, you will stay absolutely mum. Just do not draw any attention. Just watch but *do not* say a word," she cautioned me in a slow but stern voice. I agreed.

We were at the entrance to the courtyard and the people there were sitting with their back towards us. It was an unusual kind of place with different people doing varied things, just like children in a disorderly classroom before the teacher arrived.

I was curious about what they were discussing with each other, but I could hardly hear them. Suddenly another man entered from the same direction as ours. He was a very frail man with a beard, and he looked extremely worried and fearful. He brushed against my shoulder, while entering, visibly lost.

"Sorry," he said revealing his apparent panic or fear. I was not sure what he was so concerned about. He carried a big and seemingly heavy bag. I offered to help him, but he just waved his hand dismissively and walked ahead.

My attention went back to my mother who had by then reached the main front of the courtyard. She stopped to talk to a man on the left. At the same time, I saw the other man walk up straight to the few men who had been talking to each other, up on the right side. He began discussing something with them. Another man took the bag from him and went inside a room. The other men were talking to him and he seemed to be telling them how frail and weak his legs were, and how intense his pain was. I could not hear a word of what they were saying but his gestures made it apparent. It struck me that perhaps the practices of these men could treat physical ailments.

Just then my mother bent down and hurriedly started gathering the ashen soil from the ground. She stuffed it in the bag. At that instant those men helped the frail man to lie supine on the ground, with one person pouring some liquid around him. From the distance, I couldn't say for sure, but it looked like they were preparing for a ritual of sorts. Seeing the man lying down, my mother quickly tied her bag and got up. She swiftly started moving towards me, gesturing that we quickly make a move as our work there was done. Just then, I saw a blazing circle of fire around the man on the ground. He seemed to be aware of the fire and he raised his upper body to look at the fire near his feet. He then raised his legs to realize that they were drenched in the liquid. He panicked, looking at the men around as the blaze was steadily increasing. Although it was all happening behind her back, my mother looked all petrified as she hurried her steps towards me. She tried to obstruct my view as she walked, but I repositioned myself to not lose the view in the background.

Suddenly the man lying on the floor caught fire and started screaming. I was shocked. Many of the men started chanting something while the man engulfed in fire was crying and screaming in pain and agony. That's when I realized, he had been tied to the ground. My mother had reached me by then and she put a hand on my mouth and held my hand tightly, as if imploring me not to make a sound. Then she hurriedly pulled me with her, out of the rags and out of the blue gate. By this time, I was dizzy, and I don't remember crossing the road and sitting in the car, where my dad was waiting for us. We drove back home and the next thing I remember is waking up on my bed, in my room, a few hours later around dinner time.

When I got up, I was not sure if what I had experienced had been a dream or it actually happened. I was in utter disbelief that it could have been true. Just then I saw the packet of *raakh* lying on the study table in my room. My eyes widened in horror for that meant all of that had indeed happened. A man had been burnt alive in the middle of a gathering of so many people in a big house on a busy street, next to a marketplace and no one had done anything about it. The air conditioner in my room was at 18 degrees, yet there was sweat on my forehead. The face of the man when he'd accidently pushed me before meeting his fate flashed back to me. I felt a pain in my heart and my head was dizzy again. Just then my mother entered my room with a glass of water in her hand.

She sat next to me and looked calm and composed as she handed me the water. I couldn't believe her calmness. Taking the glass of water, I kept it on my side table and turned around to her, asking, "What's going on Mom? What just happened? You knew about it? Why did they kill that man? Why doesn't the police do something? Please tell me what are you hiding from me?"

My head was aching and spinning at the same time.

"I will tell you Rahul. Now that you have seen it all with your own eyes, you will believe me. Those men didn't kill that man. The man brought the oil and the matches from the market himself, to be set on fire," she said.

"What?" I gaped at her, shocked.

That's when I recalled the heavy bag he had been holding, which I offered to help him with, when he refused. He had in fact handed over that bag to one of those men.

"Yes. These men follow some old Pagan tradition where they believe it's an act of courage to choose one's own death and offer oneself to the flames. That way, their life and body become an offering to the almighty and their future lives are forgiven for they merge with the Creator. They believe when one's body starts to hurt and pain, it is a calling from the Creator that it's time for them to return to Him. They believe that it is only brave men who have the divine spark in them, who can offer themselves to the flames. They also believe one must witness themselves becoming an offering which is why the man must see his body catching fire, for that way he carries the recognition of his body dissolving into the Almighty which can only happen when one is burnt alive. "

I was shocked beyond words. I replayed the scene over and over in my mind and realized what my mother had said was indeed right. The man did give a bag probably full of oil and some other stuff to help him burn. He had been touching his legs, knees and lower body, explaining some sort of pain or weakness to the men who were talking to him. Then he had watched them light the fire. He started screaming only after his legs had caught fire. This also explained his confusion and fear during his brief encounter with me.

All of this made no sense to me. I didn't know what to say. I then noticed the packet of *raakh* on my table and quickly got up to grab it. "Ma, this is also the *raakh* of some man who chose to burn himself alive in a similar way, isn't it?" I said showing her the packet.

"Yes, Rahul, I am afraid so. I had heard about this place and what goes around here a long time ago. However, I had never attempted to go and witness it myself. When you mentioned that your friend had asked you for this *raakh*, I was shocked and worried about the kind of company you are keeping and the trap that you are getting into, in the name of spirituality. However, because you were so adamant, I realized you needed to see it to believe it."

"How can this be, ma? It doesn't make sense at all. My friend seems to be a wise guy. He talks to me about courage and sacrifice. He has taught me about the wisdom of the soul. What could be the reason for him to want this *raakh*?" I said in utter disbelief.

"He is initiating you into the tradition Rahul," my mother said with a certainty in her voice.

"What? That's not possible ma. How do you know that he's a part of this tradition?" I asked her in an exasperated tone.

"I know their ways Rahul. I was going to be initiated, when your father saved me. Last night when you mentioned wanting to go there, I decided that I would take you there. This would also enable me to face some truth of my life and bring closure to a long-unfinished story. Also, I had to ensure that you wouldn't move forward from this stage wondering whether or not what I am about to tell you is really the truth. So I opted to do this with you," she said.

"I don't understand any of this, ma. Please talk to me openly. I am not in the frame of mind to understand hints or clues, please," I said holding my head with both my hands.

"Okay, let me explain," she said putting her hand on my shoulder.

"Your father, Kamaki and I were friends. We were studying in Aligarh at the time. She and I were very thick but there was an issue. She and I both secretly loved your father. We were not completely aware of this but somehow,

I felt that she also was interested in your father. Maybe he felt it too.

She used to talk to me about life, afterlife, soul, its journey and so much other stuff that intrigued me. Your father was always very disinterested these kinds of discussions, so he kept out of it. Slowly, my trust on Kamaki and her way of looking at life grew. One day, she talked to me about the physical body and how it is a mere reflection of our soul. She also shared with me that the shortest way to attain salvation is to merge with the Creator. Upon asking her how, she said when the body starts to ache and pain, it could be an indication that the Creator is calling. That's why all old people start having body issues before they pass away. I was very naïve. I believed her because at the age of 20, it is easy for one's mind to get impressed.

In the next few weeks, I suddenly started having a lot of pain in my legs. My right leg used to hurt so much that sometimes I found it difficult to even walk straight. I had all sorts of tests done but the doctors said there was nothing wrong. I started to become extremely helpless. Your father and Kamaki were always by my side, yet, I was becoming disconnected with life since it was agonizing to live life in such excruciating pain. My parents used to live in the village while I was studying in the town, so I didn't share this with them; I didn't want them to worry about me.

One day Kamaki took me to a man who used to practice some form of the occult. I still remember his dark and gloomy room which gave me the feeling of being in a dungeon. I was petrified from the moment I entered that place, but my friend insisted that this man could help me relieve my pain. I was also desperate. I could do anything to live a normal life again.

He wore black clothes and had a long-braided beard with multi-colored beads woven into it. He was performing some ritual by putting some offerings in sacrificial fire lit in a big metallic pot next to him. We quietly went and sat opposite to him, waiting for him to open his eyes.

When he opened his eyes, he looked at both of us rather curiously and that's when Kamaki greeted him by bowing her head. She signaled me to do the same. I bowed too.

Before Kamaki could say anything, he raised his left hand and asked her to stay quiet. He was shaking the *damroo* while his eyes were closed.

Upon opening his eyes, he looked at me, "She has pain all over her body. Her legs are making her helpless. Her right leg is giving up on her. She is in agony."

Kamaki said "Yes *baba*. That's correct. Can you please help her?"

I was unsure as to how he could accurately guess my anguish without me saying a word. Just then, he spoke again. "Yes, I can help her, but she will have to trust me. I see a lot of doubt in her. I am not sure if that doubt will allow me to help her," saying which he closed his eyes again.

Just then she nudged me, as if to correct my act. I let down my guard.

He then opened his eyes again. "Will you do what I tell you to do, my child?" he asked me.

I bowed my head in acceptance.

"Okay," he said and handed me over a powder or *raakh* to apply on my legs before I took a bath each day. He also asked us to come again the subsequent week.

He closed his eyes again and Kamaki nudged me to quickly get up and move out of the room. We rushed out of the room and out of that place too. It was a sign of relief, for there was something about the place that was very suffocating.

I was not sure I believed the *baba*, but I wanted to. I hoped he would be able to help me get some respite.

I did what he asked me to and to my astonishment, my pain started to heal. I felt better and within that one week, there was tremendous improvement in my legs. I started to believe that he did after all have some powers using which he could help me when nothing else could.

We went back to him again the subsequent week and again he gave me more ashes to apply. He never charged us, so I was unsure of why he was helping me without any vested interest.

Slowly, my friend started inducting me into the old Pagan tradition where they believed that the soul used its body to traverse through a lifetime, but the body is never a part of the soul. It's like you wear clothes and then take them off when they become dirty. In this tradition, they believed that the body was an aspect of the earth, created out of the five elements and eventually it must become an offering to the fire element, for that was the element that was meant to purify the remains of the body and turn it into ashes to merge back with earth. Her elocution of the beliefs and my own relief from pain compelled me to pay attention.

All this happened while your father was unaware of

how Kamaki was turning me into a believer. In front of him, we hardly talked about this. He only knew that some *baba* helped me get rid of my pain and Kamaki had taken me to him. The nature of the information was enough to make him feel disinterested in the story.

In those days when I was in real pain, my proximity to your father was increasing. He and I had fallen in love and he was very caring and loving towards me. I think Kamaki had also started to notice this.

One day, she took me along, to witness what you witnessed today. I was fossilized. I couldn't understand how on earth this was possible. I was so taken aback that after this incident I locked myself in a room for an entire day and refused to see anyone. What I saw had shaken the entire basis of my knowledge and wisdom. I had never ever thought there were people who would be willing to burn themselves alive for the sake of merging back with the Creator. This is when I was also informed that the ashes the baba used to give me to apply on my body were those of a human being who had chosen to end his existence like this. I was so disgusted. However, I couldn't help noticing that it had worked. This realization confused me no end. Was I to accept that one must sacrifice their body or give it up at will when it starts to show signs of withdrawal since this was a sign that one was ready for their ultimate salvation? Also, that by them turning their body into ashes, the energy in those ashes becomes such that it can cure other people's aches and pains such as mine? It was all too overwhelming, but I had been a witness to it and hence couldn't deny it either.

For several days after that, I remained restless and perplexed. I chose not to share this incident with your father since I knew he would be dismayed or even upset by the both of us. I didn't intend to flare him up.

It was all too surreal. I couldn't deny it, but I couldn't accept it either. I was constantly restless and helpless at the same time, mostly as a result of over-thinking. My pain was almost healed.

One day, out of the blue, your father just came to our house when Kamaki was not at home. He was visibly frightened and concerned. He asked me to pack my bags quickly and take all my stuff. As students we lived in a minimalistic rented apartment, so I never had much except my clothes and books. I kept asking him what the matter was, but he wouldn't say a word. I suggested we wait for Kamaki to come but he insisted that we left before she came and that he would explain everything to me once we were out of the house.

I trusted him and so I abided. We went straight to the train station and hopped on a train to Delhi.

I couldn't make sense of anything, but your dad was so sure of what he was doing and so restrained that I didn't question him until we reached Delhi. His family owned a house that his grandfather had left for him when he passed away in the city. His parents lived in Mumbai; they had appointed a caretaker who was the only inhabitant of the family bungalow in Delhi.

It was when we sat in his admirable living room, had water and felt a little more relaxed that I asked him, what all of this was about.

He then told me that he had found out that Kamaki was deeply involved in a Pagan tradition where people convinced other people that they must burn themselves alive when their bodies were giving up on them. He also told me that he had come to know that these people first induce pain in one's body through occult practices and playing with their energy fields and then rescue them to impress their minds by proving their genuine intent. He reckoned Kamaki was doing something similar to me for the sake of having him to herself. She wanted to get rid of me.

I was so shocked. This is when it all made sense to me about how that *baba* had known what was wrong with me and how those ashes worked for me. I also realized how slowly I was getting trapped in the plan and I had started to believe that there is some truth to the entire thing. How they managed to do it was still a mystery to me because this did convey that there is something beyond the logical mind that has a direct bearing on one's body, but this knowledge was the least of my concerns then.

I was so gob smacked with the whole episode. I owed it to your father for saving me from burning myself alive. This was when I told him about everything that transpired between me and Kamaki and to say the least, both of us were stunned and relieved at the same time.

This was my first and only encounter with the world of spirituality and it had left such a deep and lasting impression on me that I have ever since looked away from any person even remotely spiritual.

I came to know about this tradition being followed in Bangalore too through some conversation I overheard and ever since I have refrained from stepping into that part of the city, until now.

Today, I must confess something to you Rahul. While today I saved you from exactly what I got saved all those years ago, I have realized that all these years I have judged all spiritual people for being like Kamaki. My fear was so deep that when the first time, before your marriage you confessed to me of your love for Maaya and that you were unsure if you should commit to her, I went to our local priest to ask if she was a good match for you. He told me that she had very good energies and she has chosen an intense spiritual journey in this lifetime. He also told me that she and you will share an everlasting bond and she would become the reason for you to recognize your spiritual side. The word "spirituality" was so badly stuck on the wrong side of my brain that I instantly became weary of Maaya and decided to protect you from her.

Therefore, I discouraged you from pursuing her and I was relieved that she married someone else. However, as fate would have it, you both met again, and she had a deep impact on your life again. The moment I found out that Maaya and you were together again in Delhi, I immediately sent Neha and Anushka to live with you under the pretext of saving your marriage. I must admit I chose Neha as your wife, partly also because she was as disinterested in spirituality as me.

It's only in the last few months that I met a lady who has become a close friend. She revealed to me much later into our friendship that she is also a spiritual healer. By then I had started to trust her a lot. After meeting her and understanding more about how energies work, I realized that I had limited my understanding of spirituality to only that one dark experience of my life which may have in fact been the least bit spiritual. I realized that spirituality is nothing but "recognizing the connection with one's own spirit" and it is a divine experience. However, if at a deeper level one believes in darkness and its power over the divine, they could get trapped in their own darkness while believing they were being spiritual. That is what happened to Kamaki.

I have to admit that I have been unfair to Maaya and you both. I played a role in keeping you away from her, for no fault of hers. From your craving for her and after recognizing how she has only helped you become a more loving, compassionate and trusting person, I regret my choice of judging her and becoming a reason for the two of you not being together.

Please forgive me, Rahul. I cannot sleep at night for I cannot forgive myself for what I have done in the name of a parent's love, to you. I fear I might have ruined both of your lives and Neha's too. Saying this, my mother broke down, crying profusely holding my hand.

I felt numb on the mention of Maaya. Having lost her, I was unable to come to terms with the void I felt. For a moment, I felt anger and judgement for my mother. She had no right to interfere in my life and try to control it. She had no right to judge Maaya. However, her genuine repentance changed my heart. I knew she wasn't the only one at fault. I couldn't blame her for my mistakes. I was unable to value Maaya. My mother did what she did, in her attempt to protect me from harm.

Maaya's lack of presence was changing me bit by bit. I was becoming more accepting of life. I didn't carry my aggression as my prized accomplishment anymore. I could see the other person's point of view. I could understand that each one only lives their perspective. Their point of view being different from mine didn't mean they intended to oppose me but instead maybe show me the other side of the coin. I didn't speak much. At night, I gazed at the stars, wondering what my life had become.

I allowed my mother her catharsis since I knew she had to free herself of the guilt for guiding me in a direction which brought me pain. Had I truly not wanted what she was pushing me to, I would have found ways to stop it, but I abided since I was unsure of my own choices. Soon my father joined in and he understood what had happened. He just stood there with a hand on my mother's back, caressing her, allowing her to cry her heart out. He glanced towards me with a look full of love and gratitude, mostly for allowing my mother to be free of the burden she had been carrying for ruining my life.

My parents were two souls bound in one unit. One always knew what the other was thinking and they never failed to support each other. They often made me feel like a failure for being unable to create that kind of bond in my marriage. This time however, I had finally understood that they had their own journey and their own conflicts which they were struggling with. Each one has something they are trying to go beyond, and I need not fancy someone else's perfection in one area for I might be perfect in another, and that's alright.

We ordered food from a restaurant nearby that night since my father wanted my mother not to be bothered with cooking. She was exhausted from all the crying and he wanted us to sit together and enjoy our meal together, before it was time for me to go back to Delhi.

In my mother's confession and all the events that had unfolded, I had completely forgotten about Dan and the *raakh.* When I went to sleep that night, I realized that part of Dan's involvement and his intention to initiate me into this tradition was still unaddressed. I was not sure if what my mother was saying was correct, since Dan seemed to be a nice guy. I decided to call him the next day and confront him.

The next morning, when I called him up to question him about his motives for asking for the *raakh*, Dan also seemed confused but said, "I also don't completely know the purpose Rahul. I met a guy here who has been helping me get rid of my shoulder pain which I have, ever since my wife left. He asked me to get this *raakh* so that it could help me get rid of my pain. Since you were travelling to Bangalore and my travel plans got cancelled, I thought of asking you to bring it for me. He used some of the raakh that he had, and it gave me much needed relief. That's all. Is everything okay Rahul?"

I then realized, as I had suspected that Dan also was unaware of this cult. I then explained to him the whole story and he was so stunned that his voice started to tremble. He apologized to me a few times, though it wasn't his fault either. I asked him to take care of himself and disconnected the call.

My mother was relieved to know that my friend was not directly involved.

The way this episode served my higher good was that my parents were now open to me choosing my life. I had eased my mother of the guilt that she had harbored for way too long, of her being the reason Maaya and I weren't together. I had completely succumbed to the fact that Maaya was not with me since I had yet to discover myself to be able to deserve her. Everyone who separated me from her were just playing a role in helping me realize my undeserving need for her. I had no malice against my parents and I completely understood that they operated out of their fears for me.

That night, many thoughts and images revolved in my mind and it was past one at night when I could finally sleep. No matter how much acceptance I thought I had brought of my self-discovery without Maaya, she never left my thoughts for a minute. The anxiety of travelling to Delhi and meeting Neha and Anushka added to my restlessness. The few days spent in Bangalore had been a blessing in disguise. I was surer of my choice by the time I left for Delhi.

I reached home at six in the evening, the next day. Anushka was so excited to see me. Neha offered me a glass of water while I sat on the sofa with Anushka jumping over my legs, seeking attention. Neha then busied herself with cooking dinner in the kitchen. The awkwardness between me and Neha was evident. Occasionally when Anushka called out to her, she responded from the kitchen in monosyllables. I was elated to see my little darling daughter so happy.

After putting Anushka to bed, I went to my room to sleep. Neha was already in bed and the lights were off. I was glad I didn't have to face her. The moment I lay down on the bed, she flipped over to my side and said "So, how was Singapore?"

"Singapore was great. Learnt a lot. How have you been?" I asked.

"Without you, you mean?" she taunted,

"Without me, yes, but otherwise as well. How are things at your workplace?" I tried to divert the direction in which she was headed. I was too tired to end up in an argument with her.

"Don't tell me you are so worried about my work, or even about me for that matter. Good night Rahul. You must be tired since you have had a long day. We will talk tomorrow," saying which she flipped her back and tossed to the other side. Within five minutes, I was in a deep sleep.

□

The Final Straw

I woke up to Anushka snuggling with me in bed. "Aww, my sweetie pie. Good morning," I said, kissing her on the forehead.

"Good morning papa," she said snuggling up to me while cuddling her teddy bear as well.

Soon we had tea and breakfast. It was a lazy Sunday morning and it was good to be back home. I knew there was a lot to be addressed and a lot to be taken care of, but these thoughts didn't stop me from enjoying my Sunday morning tea in our small garden while Anushka played with our dog, Folio.

She was a very happy kid and as I watched her play, I wondered if I would destroy her smile forever by separating from Neha. Something within me also assured me that she would be fine. She would always be loved by both her parents, irrespective of them living together or separate. The thought did make me uncomfortable though, and I looked away from her feeling guilty. It was the best I could do in that moment.

I was to join the Delhi Office the next day. My mind was incessantly weighed down with all that I needed to convey to Neha. I asked her if we could go for a dinner to some place nice that evening. She agreed and arranged for Anushka to spend the night at her cousin's place in Gurgaon.

We went out for dinner at "The Pavilion," Maurya Sheraton. It had always been my favorite place to dine with Maaya. I chose the same place for this dinner with Neha just so that I could muster the courage to say all that I had wanted to for so long. Neha was in a good mood. I was not sure if she had any inkling as to what I was going to say, but I was determined, nevertheless.

As we were seated by the tidily dressed waiter, he courteously asked if we'd like to be served some drinks. I looked at Neha and she agreed. Neha ordered a red wine while I ordered a single malt for myself.

Both of us sipped our drinks. There was a sudden awkwardness when it was time to spill the beans. Perhaps Neha had sensed my anxiousness, so she gave me the space to breathe by choosing to stay quiet and just watching the people passing through the corridor outside the window.

"Neha, I have thought a lot while I was in Singapore. I feel that our marriage is not working and we must part. I think I have finally come to terms with the fact that we are two completely different individuals and we tend to bring out the worst in each other," I said, looking at Neha in the eye. I wanted to finally face the situation directly.

"Hmmmm. So, what happens to Anushka? Have you thought about her too?" she retorted.

"I don't know. I guess she will always be loved by both of us, regardless of our togetherness or separation. Don't you think so?" I said.

"Really? Is it so easy? Do you think your parents will accept this decision of yours?" she enquired.

"I have talked to my parents. I went to Bangalore before I came to Delhi. I had been wanting to see them for a while", I said. Neha looked surprised and perhaps slightly hurt.

"Very well. So now your mother is alright with you and me separating? When I was ready for the separation earlier, she coaxed me into wanting otherwise," she said, sounding agitated.

"Neha, it's not for my mother or anyone else to choose for me. It's what I choose for myself. I am not able to choose you. It's not because you are a bad person or that I don't care about you or Anushka. It's just that I don't feel like I'm being myself with you. Our relationship seems like a role-play we are doing for the betterment of a common cause which is our daughter. Between us, there is hardly any connection. When I come home, I don't feel like sharing my day, my feelings, and my experiences with you. I eat what you serve me, I wear what I find in my almirah, I do as you want but that does not include my desires and choices. When I go to sleep, I don't feel like wanting to hug you or cuddling you up close to me. When I do see you in my bed at night, I want to quickly roll myself up with a pillow. I want to ensure we stay at a safe distance so that I don't have to deal with the awkwardness of the distance between us that gets thankfully hidden in the darkness of the night as soon as the lights go off. When I wake up in the morning, I don't look forward to finding you next to me in bed. Instead when I do find you, I sneak away to the bathroom so that I can get ready first without having to go through a nagging argument about whose being on time to office is more important. When I come home, I start feeling this nauseating suffocation as if I have now entered a cage that will free me for the day the following morning. The only saving grace is Anushka's smile that binds me to feeling there is a good reason why I do choose to get caged every day. I lived a liberating kind of freedom in Singapore. I came back to myself each evening and no matter how hard I worked, how much I slogged, coming back to myself, making myself a drink, cooking my own food, watching TV or reading a good book and going to sleep when my muscles needed relaxation was what gave me so much peace and contentment. Yes, sometimes I missed holding someone's hand, sharing my day, celebrating my achievements but whenever I missed that someone and closed my eyes, I didn't see your face," I said maintaining my eye contact with Neha. She seemed to be listening intently. Though her tears were flowing down her cheeks, her gaze was constant.

It took her a moment to register that I had stopped speaking. She quickly sipped her wine, kept the glass and picked up a tissue to wipe her tears.

"Whom do you see when you close your eyes, Rahul? It is Maaya, isn't it?" she said.

I was uncomfortable because I had perhaps not been prepared to talk about Maaya with Neha. We had never spoken about Maaya so openly.

"Yes, I see her. To be honest, I have never been able to replace her with you. I tried, but I have failed miserably. I am sorry Neha. I truly am. You are in this position because of my cowardice. I have failed you and Anushkha. I never meant to but that doesn't excuse me from what I have managed to do", I managed to utter without looking down.

I had finally realized that I had to go beyond my shame for my love for Maaya or the lack of my love for Neha. I had to accept myself for who I was.

"I met her last week," said Neha, to my utter shock. At first, I thought I had misunderstood her. "You met who?" I asked.

"Maaya," she said.

"What? Maaya came to meet you? Here? In India?" I asked her, anxious to know what she would say next.

"Yes Rahul. Just that she did not come to meet me. It was I who went to see her," she said.

I suddenly felt happy. It meant that Maaya was in India and that I could meet her. "Where does she live Neha? Please share her contact with me. Why did you meet her?"

Just as I uttered those words in my excitement, it occurred to me that I was talking to my wife about sharing the coordinates of my ex, with enthusiasm that could only hurt Neha. I retreated, pulling myself to rest my back in my chair.

Neha then straightened in her chair and placed her hand over mine, on the table. Looking into my eyes she said the most dreadful words.

"She is gone. She is no more Rahul. Your Maaya is dead."

It felt as if a big hammer freely falling from the sky had bumped onto my head.

"No more? What do you mean she is no more?"

I had stopped feeling the chair I was sitting on. My vision was getting blurred.

"She battled her way through cancer, Rahul and she passed away last week. Meeting me was her last wish for which the hospital called me. I went to meet her. She asked me to forgive you and to forgive herself. She said she had finally realized that your role in her life was to make her get in touch with her own self and that had been accomplished. She wanted you to know that anything other than what happened, was never meant to happen. She wanted you to forgive yourself and move on in life appreciating what you have. While I was sitting there, she started collapsing and soon the doctors lost hope. I walked out since I didn't know what else to do. I didn't have the courage to meet her family, so I just left it at that," Neha said, shedding tears for the soul who had surpassed all lessons of love and compassion through her journey.

I felt as if my life force energy had just been sucked out of me and all of it just went out of my feet, through my shoes, into the earth. I couldn't think, hear, feel or move. I couldn't bear the thought of Maaya leaving me like this. Maaya is dead, Rahul - these words kept echoing in my head. All I remember is having closed my eyes. I don't remember what happened hence.

For the longest time, I stayed numb and blank.

□

Second Wind

I was sitting on the bench in the garden in front of my room in the ashram at Auroville, wondering how two years had passed ever since I moved there. Neha and I had mutually separated and Anushka was living a happy life with her mother and stepfather. Neha had married an ex- colleague she met at a reunion and they seemed happy with each other. He treated my daughter well and she had accepted him as her father. Anushka wrote messages to me at times and we had an independent relationship which did not interfere with her life otherwise.

I had moved to the ashram in Auroville and had become a full-time volunteer there. Due to my skills as an investment banker, I volunteered to take care of their financial management and some other departments where I could be of use. In return they gave me a place to live. I ate the food that was cooked at the ashram, plus a small salary paid to me in the form of usable coupons to be used throughout the ashram.

My life was peaceful though I often missed Maaya. It took me several months to come to terms with the fact that Maaya was no more. I never had the courage to go back to

Gagan or Dev to find out what exactly had happened to her because I knew they would only blame me. I severed my ties with the world and retreated to live my life in service of others. There was peace and contentment in serving people. The void that Maaya had left in my heart was so alive that I could feel it in each breath. I had come to accept this as a part of my being.

Each day I sat in meditation and asked the creator for forgiveness for myself, for the way I treated Maaya and how I could never really give her the love she deserved. It had been two years and every few days, I would have a dream in which I would see Sarah within me, lying on the death bed with Aaron standing next to her. She called out to me. I tried to travel to her but Chazaq stopped me halfway. Each time, Chazaq and I had a sword fight. Each time, I overpowered him but the moment I'd turn my back to reach closer to Sarah, he'd hit me on my back, and I'd fall. This was when my eyes would open. No matter how many times this happened, I had never been able to reach Sarah. So many times, I even called out to Aaron for help, however, Aaron did not leave Sarah's side. He only said, "This is your battle to fight and win."

One evening, inspired by the people who were preparing for the blue moon meditation, I also decided to meditate, all by myself.

As the most spectacular blue moon showed up in the sky, I quietly walked up to my favorite spot on the rooftop of a small library building. The sky looked like a tapestry of beautifully glazed jewels hanging upside down, with the moon at the center so eloquently enhancing the grace of the cobalt blue background. It was slightly chilly with winters about to start so I had carried a warm wrap with me.

I sat down in a cross-legged position and closed my eyes. In only a few moments I treaded down the familiar path with my blood gushing towards my chest and suddenly, I found myself in front of the same cave where I used to meet Sarah. The cave still opened outwards to the snowy land. The grey dense clouds were thundering and soon, Aaron appeared. "I am glad you are back," he said.

"Are you? I thought you'd be upset with me," I said.

"No. Your return today means a lot. We must rescue Sarah. She is not doing too well. I fear for her wellbeing," he said.

"Where is she?" I asked

"She is still a captive of Chazaq. However, now I know where he lives. I can take you there. You must free Sarah from him. For that you'll have to kill him. Are you ready?" he enquired.

"Sure. Let's go."

Aaron, for the first time, shaped himself like a big bird and bent down with his back towards me. It took me a few seconds to realize he was expecting me to climb onto his back. The moment I did, he soared in the air, up above the grey skies, tearing the thunderstorms, right through the wilderness of the clouds, far-far away, holding me carefully, strong and secure, on his back. Aaron was as mighty and graceful as a bird can be. There were no colors in this winter wonderland. Even Aaron was black in color. Everywhere I looked, I saw only white snow, with shades of grey and black for the rest of the landscape.

For long we flew over several mountains and lands, through unending clouds, before we reached a dark castle lit with lots of light from all sides, standing in snow, in the middle of nowhere. Aaron flew till the gate of the castle and then flew down to touch the ground before offloading me. He then quickly changed back his shape to the grey cloud, "From here Rahul, it's your role to play. If you can save Sarah today, you will learn your chosen lesson for this lifetime and your destiny shall then become whatever you choose to create of it. If you lose today, you shall then have to work through several lifetimes to bring her back from where she will be carried away by Chazaq. Her death in this realm will not finish her but her separation from you will be a distance you might take several lifetimes to cover. You have trusted me to bring you till here, so you are realizing the power of your choices and your wisdom. I am afraid, this is your only chance of retrieving whatever you have lost so far. Go, and always remember, Chazaq is also created from the same thread as you because he is but a manifestation of your ego. The only way to win over Chazaq is to allow yourself to be brutally honest about yourself and face your fears. Anything that you try to hide, deny or cover up about yourself will empower him. The more aligned you are with your true being, the lesser the chance of Chazaq's survival in your energies. He thrives on your darkness. As you become aligned with who you truly are, the light within you will dismantle him."

I quickly started moving towards the castle on foot. As I ran towards the main gate, it opened automatically. As I entered the main door, I found myself in a big empty hall.

It was so dark, yet the moonlight coming from the sky was showing me a glimpse of the hall which bore a haunting look in bluish grey hues. It was damp and cold.

I didn't know what to do and where to look for Sarah. I was not sure if calling out her name was a good idea. The place was intensely silent and unnerving. I could hear my own heartbeat.

"Rahul...." I heard Sarah call me. Her voice was full of pain. "Rahul, I am here. Come closer to me. Come forward," I heard.

As I valiantly stepped ahead, my movement was obstructed by a glass wall. Sarah was lying on the other side of that glass wall. She was lying with her back on a stone slab with her left hand sloppily falling off the slab. She attempted to lift her upper body, turning towards me, beckoning me towards herself. There was so much agony and feebleness in her eyes.

There was no way through the glass wall to the other side. It was a plain wall with no door for me to reach Sarah. I was perplexed and anxious. I didn't know what to do next.

"Sarah, how can I reach you? There is no way through this glass." I screamed out for my voice to reach her.

"Hello my master! I am Chazaq. Welcome to my castle. I have avoided this day forever, but I guess it's time now," I heard a husky firm male voice out of nowhere.

"Where are you Chazaq? Why can't I see you?" I enquired.

"I am this wall that you see ahead of you. You can see through me, but you cannot go beyond me. You have built this wall between yourself and Sarah. Now my existence is rooted in it. I can allow you to see her, but I cannot allow you to reach her. If you do, I will be dissolved forever and that I shall not allow," I heard.

That's when I realized that Aaron was right. My ego had become so powerful that it had developed an identity of its own. It was created through my fears and my resistances and now, it had built a kingdom inside me where it ruled. What was this kingdom anyway? If all of this was me, what exactly was Chazaq doing inside me? How did he play a role in my life, I wondered?

"He creates fears inside you, Rahul," I heard someone whisper in my left ear. Surprised as I started to look towards my left, I heard the voice again.

"I am Aaron. I have come with you. I am hiding in your collar. Do not reveal me. I shall guide you here, for that's my role to play. My voice might seem like a whisper but if you pay enough attention, I will be able to help you cross that wall, Rahul."

There was a sense of relief inside me. I was glad to know that no matter how much Aaron disapproved of me, he was still there for me.

"Listen carefully, Rahul. I can talk to you within your mind. You will just need to stay focused on me. Chazaq has built this kingdom based on your ego, which in turn is based on your fears. Only those who are fearful from inside defend themselves through their ego. The problem is not the ego, but that you are being controlled internally by your fears and they have become the driving force of your life. You cannot be driven by your fears any longer. It's time for you to be driven by self-belief instead," I heard him say.

Within my mind, I responded to Aaron, "So how do I reach Sarah? How can I go beyond this wall?"

"Do you see that yellow line near your foot?" Aaron asked.

As I looked down, I saw a shining yellow line near my feet, just before the glass.

"The moment you step on it, all your fears will come alive. That is when you will truly step into Chazaq's domain. He will apply all his might to scare you, make you feel weak and compel you to withdraw. You must face each fear Rahul. Just be brave. Trust me. Just keep trusting me and yourself. This is where your belief in love, in Maaya and in your wisdom will play a role. I cannot help you beyond this line for it is me who will also be renewed if you do in fact go beyond this line," Aaron said.

The mere mention of Maaya at this time made me feel sad. Just then I told myself that I could not let Sarah die, the way I let Maaya die. I was ready to take on Chazaq because now I was prepared to fight and reclaim my world.

Just then I asked, "And if I don't? If I cannot? What if I fail?"

There was no response. Absolute silence.

I took a long, deep breath. I knew I had no choice. This was it. I had to face it. With conviction in myself, I stepped over the yellow line.

I heard a big roar, almost as if I had stepped on the tail of a dragon. Suddenly everything around me started flying away. As I looked at the glass ahead of me, it turned into a mirror and what I saw of myself was like a manifestation of my worst nightmare. My body started turning snakelike from head to toe. Horns were growing on my head. My teeth grew big like that of a vampire and I growled and howled like a blood sucking beast. The darkness and ruthlessness in my being grew so much that I felt pain in my heart, as if the devil inside me was tearing my chest apart and revealing itself. Sarah started to scream. Soon she was on fire. She was burning alive in front of me. She was pleading for help. The flames were consuming her right in front of my eyes and I could do nothing because no matter what I did, I couldn't move my feet away from the yellow line. I was stuck with my feet frozen in that position. My inner devil was immensely powerful, and it was consuming me. My blood was boiling. My hands had grown monstrous. Snakes hissed in my ears; they told me I had to kill Sarah to survive. I was using all my strength to keep myself in check.

Demonic thoughts overwhelmed me. "No one is mine... Sarah abandoned me and so did Maaya. They don't deserve a place in my heart. My love is reserved for only myself. I need nobody. I care about no body. Everyone is selfish. All I must do is to protect myself from hurt and pain. Sarah is the root to all my pain. I must destroy her before the pain destroys me." I felt a rage developing in me which controlled my hands. I was antagonistically banging the glass and it was developing cracks. A dark force inside me wanted to break the glass to make sure I put an end to Sarah. Another side of me was deeply anguished listening to her pleas for help. I was at war with myself and I was unsure of who I was.

Just then, my thoughts went to Aaron. In all the chaos, I remembered that Aaron told me that he was always with me. I just needed to focus on him to hear him.

"Aaron, are you there? Save Sarah please..." I found myself desperately screaming out in my mind to Aaron.

"Allow her to burn. Watch her burn. Watch your own darkness. Do not panic. Just be. Close your eyes. Witness your darkness within. Let it take over you. Let it experience you fully. Let yourself be consumed by it. Do not fight it. Do not get anxious. Remember you are not this darkness. It is an illusion. You are the light. You have your own light. Seek your light while being surrounded by this darkness," I heard Aaron guiding me.

With a searing pain in my heart, I followed Aaron's advice and closed my eyes to Sarah. I allowed whatever was happening to just happen. I allowed the darkness to consume me. It felt as if reptiles were sneaking up my body and feeding on every muscle I had. An eerie presence was creeping all over my body, into each cell of my being, as if everything was ending. Everything seemed to be melting with the darkness spilling out of me. It was like molten lava that just dissolved and destroyed anything and everything that came in its way. Sarah's screams were growing louder. She was calling out to me for help. I was so helpless and broken in my spirit that my head was spinning. Each time I heard Sarah, I felt a dagger pierce through my heart, shredding it into a million pieces. A trace started to settle in amidst the perplexing experiences happening all at once. I was sliding through a tunnel, deep inside myself to somewhere beyond the darkness. I crossed rivers and valleys of the fiery red lava that was burning everything in me. Finally, I was standing in a sea of the lava atop a rock. Till wherever my sight went, all I saw was red sweltering lava. I then noticed a big shiny object floating near my feet. It drew my attention.

"Pick it up Rahul. That's the seed of light inside you," I heard Aaron talk to me.

As I bent forward to pick up the shiny object, I saw it up close. It was a big geometrical diamond like crystal emanating golden sparkle coming from within. The moment I touched it, I fell back with a jerk as if some sort of electric current pushed me away. I was scared to touch it again for if I fell from the rock on which I had carefully balanced my feet, I was bound to fall in the lava. The heat coming out of the surroundings was not helping me either.

Just then I recalled that Aaron said it was all an illusion to test my trust on my inner light. I extended my hand and touched the gemstone, carefully lifting it out of the molten lava. It hurt a bit, but my grip was strong. A sharp current came out of the diamond which threw me off-balance again but this time I didn't let it slip away from my hands. As I tightened my grip around it, it stabilized in my hand and I was able to hold it and close my fist.

Suddenly the chaos, the lava, the noises, the heat, the flames, everything started receding. When I felt the stone was stable in my hands, I slowly opened my grip to see it. It opened to a goblet shaped third eye with newly opening wings. Its wings started fluttering and it soon flew out of my hands into the sky and started manifesting into a beautiful giant bird.

It flew high with the might of its wings, constantly fluttering, till I witnessed a magnificent phoenix emerging out of it.

The most beautiful sight,

With all his might,

He emerged out of the ashes,

Away he flew,

He was stunning,

Oh, so beautiful!

He was wild as the flames,

He was bright as the golden light,

He could scream and roar,

He could fly galore,

He was my wisdom being set free,

He was my spirit revealing its light,

He was the phoenix king,

He was Aaron with his magnificent wings,

He got back his color and his valor,

My body turned golden,

The lava disappeared,

The skies became clear,

The snow was all gone,

The bright sun shone,

I sat on him and off we flew,

Beyond the mountains, beyond the skies,
To Sarah he took me, the gigantic Aaron,
There she lay, on her slay,
She was dressed in a pristine white gown,
Chazaq's glass was broken,
Sarah was renewed free,
She joined me on Aaron's sturdy back,
Together we flew, beyond the bounds of time,
Higher and higher we rose together,
All of us unified
Rejoicing the reign of the magnanimous Aaron,
For the light had risen again... forever and ever!

I finally found some closure within and it felt as if some very old and deep burden was lifted off my chest. Feeling lighter and more energetic after a long time was a welcome feeling, I realized how uplifting it was to finally embrace Sarah-my inner feminine energy.

The next day I decided to go back and visit my parents. I had not been in touch with anyone ever since I had moved to Auroville. I had never even told anyone as to where I was. I just called my parents or Anushka from a public phone booth whenever I wanted to speak to them. There was no way for them to contact me though. I had completely disengaged from everyone I knew, to only be with self.

Some sort of veil had lifted, and I felt free and joyful for no reason. Nothing in my life had changed physically, but I felt blissful inside. I found myself smiling all the time for no apparent reason.

From the money I had in my bank account that had just been lying there ever since I started living in Auroville, I bought a ticket for myself from Chennai to Bangalore. I gratefully accepted the lift I was offered to Chennai by a family who was leaving the ashram that morning after a week-long stay.

On the flight, I managed to get an aisle seat. The leg space was ample, and the seat was comfortable enough for me to sleep throughout the duration of it. I had woken up at wee hours that morning, so I slept soundly. A hand touched me gently on my right shoulder. It was the girl on the middle seat. She wanted to go to the lavatory. She had no choice but to coax me to get up. I got up, allowing her space to leave. I had to wait for her to return so that she could get back in. While wondering what to do, my eyes fell on a book she had been reading. It was lying open, upside down, perhaps for her to identify where she left it.

The author's name on the back cover caught my attention. It said "Maaya." I impulsively picked up her book, curious to read the blurb.

"Athletes are found to reach top performance through the second gush of wind that comes rushing into their system after completely losing breath once. Maaya experienced this too, when death came face-to-face with her, and renewed her life. *Second Wind* is the story of Maaya, of how she got a fresh lease of life post her battle with Cancer in 2017, through a near death experience.

It was her second wind that gave her another chance to live, but with renewed purpose. Maaya is now a healer, therapist and writer who believes her life's purpose is to help souls find themselves by going beyond their innate fears and recognizing their inner light which sits deep within the darkness of their ego. Maaya reckons that each one of us is capable of infinite bliss and compassion, and all it takes to uncover the potential within is recognition that all the darkness, all the fears that we believe are real are actually, mere illusions created by our ego to ensure we never trust our innate power.

Maaya lives in Bangalore and can be reached at maaya@gmail.com"

My already racing heart palpitated even more when I read a phone number mentioned below the website. I was so perplexed reading the back cover that my mind was not completely with me. Just then my eyes fell on the picture of the author.

It was Maaya! My Maaya. She was wearing a red saree and looked as graceful as ever.

I couldn't believe what had just happened. My hands were trembling as tears rolled down my eyes. It was Maaya! She was alive! "Oh my God! Oh my God! Thank you... God!"

My heart was racing like never before. Such a flood of mixed emotions arose in me that I didn't know how to hold myself in my seat. I used one of my hands to cover my mouth else I could have screamed in delight. Just then the girl returned from the lavatory. I got up, gave her the seat, handed over her book to her and gave her a kiss on her forehead. My teary-eyed face perhaps nipped in the bud any offence she may have otherwise taken to my sudden affection for her.

I quickly rushed to the lavatory and for a few moments I just looked at myself in the mirror and cried. These were tears of happiness, of joy, of ecstasy.

It no longer mattered to me whether Maaya and I could have a life together or not. The fact that she was alive was blessing enough for me. All I now wanted was to hear her voice just once.

Soon, the flight's descent was announced.

I was so restless in my excitement that it took me three attempts to fix the safety belt on my waist. The girl next to me was baffled with my behavior. I was unable to express anything I was feeling in words because I was sure that even if I tried to speak, no words would leave my mouth. This was the first time in two years that I regretted not possessing a mobile phone anymore.

I contemplated what I would say when I talked to her or met her. It occurred to me that she may not want to see me. I wondered what I would do then. Just when I was again trapping myself in my fears and doubts, I heard a familiar whisper saying, "Cross the bridge when you come to it."

As soon as we got off the plane, I rushed to locate a phone booth in the airport. Choosing to pick my luggage from the luggage belt later, the first thing I wanted to do was to call Maaya.

Upon finally finding a phone booth, I quickly dialed the number I had memorized from the back of the book.

"Hello..." I heard the voice recording play and pushed a coin inside the phone booth.

"Hello, this is Maaya here, may I know who's speaking?"

I was so overwhelmed because it was indeed her voice.

"Maaya, it's me!" I said.

"Rahul... is it you?" I heard.

Life had indeed, come full circle.

□□□

Minal Arora

Minal is a technocrat turned Healer, Mentor and Author. After successfully playing different roles in her career, she finally moved on from the position of the CEO of an IT company, in her quest to explore the side of her that sought love over conflicts, compassion over control, universal logic over coding logic and acceptance over deliverance.

She lives in Delhi NCR, India and inspires people to heal themselves of the inner conflicts they carry, thus recognising themselves anew. Her vast life experience as a therapist and mentor lends her a unique perspective on human life, growth, relationships, and situations. Her connection with her own higher consciousness enables her to guide people seeking love, peace and fulfilment in their lives whilst living their roles and responsibilities in the best way.

Minal conducts Serenity Surrender (SS) Healing Workshops to teach self-healing to those who are keen to transform their lives such that they can truly fulfil their higher purpose.

You can read more about Minal on www.pastlifeconnection.com or write to her at minal_arora@yahoo.com

Maaya: A tryst with Self (Prequel to Second Wind)
Discover the story of Maaya, through Minal Arora's
"Maaya: A tryst with self"